HOPE

Published by WordCrafts Press
Cody, Wyoming 82834
www.wordcrafts.net

Hope

Abby Rosser

WordCrafts

Contents

DEDICATION

For Owen;
"The possible's slow fuse is lit by the Imagination."
-Emily Dickinson

JENNY

No matter that she had been in this strange skin for 100 years or more, Jenny still had to remind herself how to walk and move and be. Her steps were sluggish bounces. When she moved her hands, it was as if her fingers were underwater and pulling against a strong current.

The daytime noises buzzing around her—mostly bird calls and chirping bugs—were too quiet. They sounded muffled, as if she were wearing her wool cap with the furred ear flaps snuggly in place. But she no longer wore her wool cap, nor any other hat or mittens or shoes or stockings, for that matter. Her clothes were the same in every season: her pink and green gingham dress and a white pinafore. A curly *J* was embroidered on the pocket of her pinafore, her mother's stitches smooth and sure.

The nighttime noises were a different thing all together. Jenny wished she could silence the snarling growls and the piercing wails and the wretched weeping sounds that always seemed just inches away. She waited out the nights in tree branches, hiding amongst the leaves.

Jenny spent her days searching for patches of sunshine. When she found one, she would arrange herself on a rock or a grassy spot or even at the tippy-top of a bending pine tree and just try to *be* the sunshine. She would close her eyes and tilt her face to the sky. Jenny would swallow the sun's rays if she could because she was tired of feeling cold all the time, just like she was tired of being invisible and tired of feeling afraid.

But mostly she was tired of being alone.

SUNDAY

One

SUMMER CAMP

"Never stand up in a canoe," Dooley's father said.

"And don't drink out of the lake. I'm sure that water is filthy," his mother added.

"I've got it," Dooley answered. His parents were on hour three of camp advice, and he didn't think he could take much more.

When his neighbor Cyrano had told him about Camp Pukwudgee, the camp for magically gifted kids, Dooley couldn't believe his luck. But before he could go, he had to explain to his parents about Cyrano's magical family and his own supernatural power as a Visus, someone who can see things that others can't. It was a long conversation which spanned several days, but his parents' reaction had surprised him when they eventually said he could go to camp.

"And then there are the mosquitoes," Dooley's mother turned around to look at him in the backseat of the minivan, "You did pack bug spray, didn't you?"

"Yes, mom. I've got everything. I *promise*."

"Magic powers or no magic powers, mosquitoes carry diseases. Cyrano being able to *smell the future*," she said, using quote fingers, "won't save you from West Nile Virus."

His mother turned back around to face the front, mostly satisfied with Dooley's answer and his level of mosquito defense.

"Paul, are you sure this is the way the map said to go?" She smoothed the paper in her lap and squinted at the lines and symbols. The country road they had been traveling looked more suited for horse-drawn wagons than cars.

"Yes. It said to take this road until it forks."

The van bounced over a rut, propelling some of the items in Dooley's brand new backpack into the air and onto the floor of the van. Faintly gleaming beneath a few pencils, a handful of wrapped candies and a flashlight was Dooley's compass. He picked it up, his heart pounding at the thought of losing or breaking this connection to his recent adventures with Cyrano. He held it for a moment, watching the needle spin lazily around the face.

Where do I want to go? Dooley thought to himself. The compass was bewitched to always reveal the direction the bearer wished to go. When Dooley used the compass a few weeks ago, it showed no regard for actual cardinal directions like a normal compass. Instead, the letters would shift around the dial and the needle would spin until it pointed North, and he and Cyrano would walk in the indicated direction. That small brass instrument had led them through dark tunnels of an enchanted fortress, helping them succeed in their plan to rescue a family of cursed creatures. Dooley sighed. He carefully zipped it inside the front pocket of his backpack and patted the round outline.

"Okay, we're supposed to turn left at what looks like a one-eyed rooster," his mom said, squinting down at the tiny picture on the map.

"It's a good thing the camp sent a map, Dooley," said his father as he glanced at Dooley in the rearview mirror. "We never would've found this place. It's not on any of the other maps I looked at."

Seconds later, the road split into a **V**, separating in opposite directions. Just where it split there stood a giant metal sculpture. The creature had outstretched wings and an opened, curved beak with rows of sharp teeth. It had one disproportionately large eye just above the beak.

"I guess that's it," his mom said. "Turn left here on Snallygaster Road."

Dooley stared out the window at the surrounding woods, nervous excitement bubbling inside him. He was about to meet other kids like him, kids with powers and special abilities. He was relieved that Cyrano and two of Cyrano's sisters were also attending camp.

Dooley's father slowed his driving as the road became even more rough nearer the entrance to the camp. Dooley noticed a break in the woods. One section of the thick mass of trees was replaced by a rock the size of a doghouse. He spotted a young, red-headed girl sunning herself on the rock. She was lying on her back with one arm dangling by her side and one arm resting over her eyes.

"Huh, that's weird," Dooley said as he watched the girl.

"What's weird?" his mom asked.

"That girl. She looks like she's out of *The Little House on the Prairie* or something."

"What girl?"

"The one on the rock; the girl with the old-timey pink and green dress. Didn't you see her?"

"We're here," his father announced before Dooley could further describe the girl. "Let's go get you checked in."

Two

CABIN CALL

"**L**eo Johnson. Jackalope Cabin." A man with a bright red collared shirt tucked neatly into his khaki shorts stood below a flagpole and read from a clipboard. Every hair on his strawberry-blond head and in his strawberry-blond moustache was in place. "Tosh and Tut Nelson. Gumberoo."

Dooley saw a group standing in a circle as he and his parents approached. Each time the man read another name, a camper would peel away from the group, dragging a duffel bag or suitcase to walk toward a cabin.

Dooley saw Cyrano standing on the opposite side of the circle.

"Dooley, over here," Cyrano said in a loud whisper as he waved frantically in their direction.

Dooley and his parents joined Cyrano and his family.

"Clio already knows she's in the Wendigo Cabin. We're just waiting to hear about me and Celeste."

"It's my first time to go to camp," Cyrano's eight-year-old

sister Celeste told Dooley. She was gripping her mom's hand uneasily.

"Me, too," Dooley reassured her.

"Sama Rahal. Wendigo Cabin."

Cyrano's sister Clio squealed and hugged the girl standing next to her.

"Three years in a row to be in Cabin Wendigo!" Clio cheered as the two girls performed a complicated handshake that culminated in bumping their rear ends together. "Clio and Sama! Soul Sisters! Best Chums! We stick together no matter what comes!"

Dooley leaned toward his mom and whispered, "Remember how I told you that Clio can only speak in rhymes?" He pointed to Clio with his thumb. "That's what I was talking about."

His mom nodded in acknowledgment.

"Celeste Mulligan. Hodag Cabin. Cyrano Mulligan. Jackalope Cabin."

"Well, that's me," Cyrano said to Dooley as he gathered his belongings. "Good luck."

"Beryl Fletcher and Tristen Bergman. Rougarou Cabin."

Dooley watched as one girl with waist-length blond hair and big blue eyes lightly tapped another girl with chestnut brown skin and purple dreadlocks on the arm, then the first girl began to gesture with hand signs. As the second girl signed back in response, Dooley noticed that each of her fingernails was painted a different color.

"That's Beryl. She's deaf," said a boy to Dooley's right. He wore a shirt with a picture of a Mohawk-topped

Shakespeare wearing headphones. "I'm a Vox, so I could translate for her if I wanted to—but I don't feel like it."

"A Vox?" Dooley asked.

"A Voice. A Translator. I speak like hundreds of languages."

"Oh, Right. I'm Dooley."

"Virgil. You're Cyrano's friend, aren't you?"

"Yeah. We're neighbors."

"You're a Visus, right?"

"Yep."

"*Mahusay*. That's 'excellent' in Filipino. I've never met a Visus before."

Dooley just nodded. He wasn't sure how to respond to this older boy who was obviously cooler than him in every way.

Clipboard man continued reading: "Virgil Lee. Waheela."

Virgil put on his sunglasses. "*Farxad*. That's 'goodbye' in Somali."

When the man with the clipboard had read all of the names, he looked around to see Dooley and his parents still standing and waiting.

"Hi there. I'm Busby Danner, head counselor. Can I help you?" he asked.

"I'm Dooley Creed. I just signed up for camp last week?"

"Dooley Creed. Dooley Creed." Busby flipped through the papers on his clipboard. "Oh yes, latecomer. There's an extra bed in Jackalope or you could bunk with Smitty." He looked up from his papers and chuckled to himself.

"Smitty?" Dooley's mother asked.

"The Lake Monster," he answered, smoothing down his moustache hairs which were already in perfect order.

"Lake Monster?" his mother gasped, "How is it safe to have a monster…"

"The Jackalope Cabin sounds perfect," his father interrupted. Dooley and his father jostled his mother toward the boys' cabins before she could change her mind about the whole thing.

Three

JACKALOPES

It took him a few minutes, but Dooley eventually convinced his parents to say their goodbyes outside his cabin. His mother was on the verge of launching a full home inspection of the building, so he had to promise to write home as often as possible with loads of details about his experiences. Once they were gone, he climbed the worn wooden steps and opened the door of the Jackalope Cabin, inhaling the earthy blend of pine trees, mildew and sweaty boys from the cabin's decades of summer camps.

"Body of a hare with antlers on its head," its inhabitants sang out with energetic motions, "Kick you in the face and make you wish you're dead! We are Jackalopes. We never go to bed!"

"Dooley!" Cyrano happily punched his friend's arm. "I was worried they'd put you in the Gumberoo Cabin with the 8-year olds! Come on. I think there's a bottom bunk over here by Leo."

Cyrano brought Dooley to the back of the cabin to show him the last empty bed. "That's Leo," Cyrano said as he pointed to a boy sitting on the upper bunk, looking out the window towards the girls' cabins.

Leo was sitting cross-legged with his elbows on his knees and his chin resting on his fists. A paintbrush was situated behind his ear.

"Dude, she's not worth it," Cyrano told Leo. "Girls are way too much trouble. Believe me—I have four sisters."

"What's he doing?" Dooley asked.

"You know those artistic types—always *in love*," Cyrano muttered.

"Come on, Cyrano, even a grouch like you can see how perfect we'd be together. Me, a Brush, and Beryl, a Palette."

"So I remember what a Brush is—someone who can paint pictures that come to life, like that sun your great-granddad painted that gave off sunshine even though he was underground," Dooley whispered to Cyrano. "But what's a Palette?"

"Beryl is actually a telepath," Cyrano explained. "She can use her mind to speak to other people's minds when they're hypnotized or asleep or just really focused or something."

"But she's extra amazing because she can also sense vibrations coming from colors," Leo said as he hopped down from the top bunk. "With her eyes closed, she can feel heat from a vermilion orange and watery depth to an aqua blue. Can you imagine if a Brush had that kind of power?"

"Remember what happened when you made that sculpture of Beryl's head in the craft shack last year?" Cyrano asked. "It was made out of dry noodles and beans, glued together and painted to look like her."

"I was experimenting with new mediums."

"Yeah, well, Clio said a rainmaker spell: '*Rain come down on that noodle/bean goop; make it a wet and soggy soup.*'"

"Yes. Don't remind me. That was so embarrassing."

"Then you made a sock puppet that looked like *sort of* like Beryl…" Cyrano began.

"Okay, I get it!"

"You're a Brush, so why didn't you just *paint* a picture of her?" Dooley asked.

Cyrano looked down at his shoes, causing his glasses to slip down his long nose, waiting to see if Leo would answer.

"It's just that I'm not a very good painter, so I don't know what would happen."

"If you're not very good at painting," Dooley tried to ask delicately, "How do you know that's your power?"

"All campers report to the lodge in five minutes," Counselor Busby shouted through a megaphone just outside the cabin.

"When I was eight, a Namer told my parents that I was a Brush," Leo explained as the boys walked toward the door. "That was just before I came to Camp Pukwudgee for the first time. Then while I was here I painted a picture that showed that the Namer was actually right, but now… now I'm not so sure."

"What do you mean?" Dooley wondered. "What was the picture you painted?"

"You ever heard of a Squonk?" asked Leo.

"No," Dooley answered.

"There's this legend about them—stories that all the counselors tell the campers—but nobody living had ever seen a Squonk in person," answered Leo. "That is, until I painted one five years ago."

"The same thing happened with the Teakettler you painted," Cyrano volunteered. "And now we hear it whistling, somewhere out there—at night—in the Bloodstone Forest."

"You guys are just trying to scare me. I mean Squonks and Teakettlers? Come on."

Leo gave Dooley a friendly slap on the back. "I only wish we were making this up, man. Just pray you don't have a reason to go out at night. Then you'll find out what's really real."

Four

SAFETY SEMINAR

"Settle down, campers. Settle down," Counselor Busby attempted to get everyone quiet enough to start his First Day of Camp Lecture. "We've got a lot to cover before we can get started on all the fun. Now I know that most of you have been to Camp Pukwudgee before, but we can never be too prepared when it comes safety." He took this moment to put on a red ball cap that read SAFETY PATROL in clear black letters. "Isn't that right, Tosh and Tut?" Busby was looking towards the front row at a set of identical twins.

"Yes, Counselor Busby," the boys said in embarrassed unison.

"Those are the Nelson twins," whispered Cyrano. "They're Ants."

"Ants?" Dooley asked.

"Yeah, tiny but incredibly strong. Last year was their first year at camp, and I guess they felt like they had to show off—being the smallest kids here and everything—so they tried to drag Smitty from the Lake."

"Smitty, the Lake Monster?" Dooley said a little too loudly.

"Shh," Cyrano scolded, gesturing toward Busby and his ongoing presentation.

"This portion of my Camp Safety Seminar I call: 'Friend or Foe? Seventeen Creatures to Avoid in the Bloodstone Forest...'" Busby continued. He indicated to a stack of posters sitting on the horizontal bar of an easel to his left.

"Smitty's pretty gentle as long as he's left alone," Cyrano explained. "But the Nelson twins grabbed him by the tail and started pulling him out of the lake. Smitty really didn't have a choice but to attack. He thrashed his tail back and forth until the boys let go. They went flying into some trees. Tosh and Tut had to go home early with broken bones."

"...which brings me to number four: The Gowrow. If you see one of these tusked reptiles, back away slowly while simultaneously humming 'Camptown Races' and never break eye contact. Gowrows are easily intimidated by staring contests, and they have a strong aversion to American folk songs written by Stephen Foster." Busby switched to his next poster and droned on with his list.

"So, should I be worried?" Dooley whispered to Cyrano.

"Worried about what?"

"Lake monsters and the Bloodstone Forest and creatures that you have to hum songs at to escape?"

"Dooley, you battled a Valkyrie and lived to tell about it. I think you'll be fine."

"So these creatures that Busby is warning us about, they're not really dangerous?"

"Any wild animals are dangerous," Cyrano argued. "You just have to use common sense."

"So that creature that Leo painted…"

"The Squonk," Cyrano offered.

"Right, the Squonk. It's not going to attack us or anything?"

"It's hard to say. A Squonk is pretty shy, and they cry a lot for some reason. Maybe it's because they're covered in warts and they're embarrassed about how ugly they are. They're supposed to be good at finding lost things. If you can find the Squonk first, that is. When Leo painted one, it just leapt off his canvas and ran away before anyone could do anything about it. Apparently, they're really hard to catch. They can disappear, and then all that's left is a puddle. Then they just show up somewhere else."

"So what's the big deal about Leo painting one?"

"No one ever knew for sure if they were real. It was just stories about Squonks. Then Leo created one. We're just not sure if he made a Boy Squonk or a Girl Squonk, and—if you had one of each they would…you know…" Cyrano's voice trailed off.

"Make baby Squonks?" Dooley added helpfully.

"Yes, and then we'd be in trouble because they would take over the place."

"Gotcha," Dooley answered, in part to stop Cyrano from feeling like he had to explain anymore about how Baby Squonks are made.

"There is one other thing about Squonks," Cyrano

remembered. "They are attracted to hard candy, and if they get some, they go berserk."

"And number 17," Busby concluded, "The Wampus. This half cat/half woman creature is nocturnal, and she's known for her intense howling and sharp claws. My best advice is to steer clear of her. She is strong enough to break bones, and from my own personal experience," Busby choked a bit on his last words, "to break hearts. A-hem. Campers, I apologize for the long lecture and the late start to supper." *Sniff.* "Dismissed."

"Okay, what was that about?" Dooley asked Cyrano and Leo as they stood up to leave the meeting lodge.

"Now that is a great story," answered Leo. "A story of forbidden love. Pain delivered in response to affection!"

"Ugh," said Cyrano, "Here we go again with the love stuff! Counselor Busby had a crush on a Wampus, but it turns out that he has a cat allergy. The end. Let's go eat."

Five

GHOST GIRL

As they stood in line to enter the mess hall, Dooley noticed the same girl he had seen by the side of the road, sunning herself on a rock. Now she sat in a patch of clover, weaving her long red hair into a thick braid and tying the end with a piece of coarse twine. When the girl looked at Dooley, something crumpled inside him and pricked him just behind his eyes. Dooley saw a remote sadness written on her face, so he gave her a small friendly wave.

"Who are you waving at?" Cyrano asked.

"That girl over there." Dooley pointed at her. "She looks, I dunno, lonely."

The girl swung herself up to her feet in one swift motion and hurried to where Dooley stood in the line of campers. She was moving her lips, but Dooley could hear no sounds.

Sama and Clio were in line just in front of Dooley. "Did you say something?" Sama turned around to ask Dooley.

"What?"

"Just now," Sama closed her eyes and cocked her head to one side. "I heard a voice."

The girl was standing right next to Dooley now.

"Maybe it was her," Dooley said. "Did you say something?" The girl continued to try to communicate with Dooley.

"Dooley," Cyrano asked, "who are you talking to?"

"Her."

"You can see me," Sama spoke with her eyes shut tight. "I hear a voice saying, 'You can see me.'"

"There's no one there," said Cyrano. He waved his hand in the general space where the girl stood, and Dooley watched as Cyrano's fingers went right through her cheek like she was made of air.

"Oh!" Dooley gasped.

"Now the voice is saying something else," said Sama. "It says, 'My name is Jenny.'"

Dooley watched as the girl turned her head in the direction of the setting sun.

"Jenny," Dooley said, reaching out his hand to her.

She nodded. Just as she began to lay her hand on his, a high-pitched whistle sounded from the forest behind them. Dooley jumped.

"It's only the Teakettler making its nightly sound," Clio said to comfort the startled Dooley. "No need to fear that backward-walking hound."

Jenny turned from the group and ran toward the forest.

"Wait! Come back!" Dooley yelled.

"She said, 'I'll find you,'" Sama repeated as Dooley watched Jenny disappear into the darkening shadows.

After they sat down on the bench with their fellow Jack-alope campers, placing their plastic cafeteria trays on the long wooden table, Dooley and Cyrano continued their discussion about the strange girl only Dooley could see and only Sama could hear.

"So Jenny is a… what?" Cyrano wondered aloud, then dropped his voice to a whisper. "A ghost?"

"I guess so. That's possible, right?" Dooley asked.

"There are all kinds of legends and stories about Camp Pukwudgee. But I've never heard of one about a ghost camper named Jenny."

"And I'm guessing Clio's friend could hear Jenny because she can hear things no one else can hear, like how I can see things other people can't see," Dooley asked.

"Yes," Cyrano explained, "Sama is a Locito. So basically she's an eavesdropper. She can hear things happening far away or really quiet things." He stabbed a green bean with his fork and sniffed it before putting it in his mouth. He continued talking while chewing, "And it looks like Sama can hear dead people, too."

Leo, who had been sitting near the Rougarou Cabin's table to stealthily watch Beryl, threw away his trash and added his tray to the stack, then scanned the mess hall for Dooley. He smiled and made a beeline to where the boys sat. "So, Dooley, I heard you already have a girlfriend. They say she's to die for!"

"Ha. Ha. Very funny, Leo," Dooley replied. He stood to leave though he had barely eaten.

"There's a rumor she's a real angel," Leo continued.

"Cut it out," Cyrano said, following Dooley to the door. "It's not funny."

"Come on. I'm just kidding," Leo claimed. "Don't be mad."

When the three boys were back outside walking to their cabin, Dooley said, "It's weird, but I can't help feeling sorry for her. She seems sad, and she definitely looked scared when she heard that Teakettler thing. I want to help her, but I don't know how."

Cyrano clapped his friend on the back. "Well, Jenny the Ghost Girl said she'd find you. So you probably just have to wait and see."

MONDAY

Six

GEMINUS

When Dooley woke up early the next morning after a nearly sleepless night spent listening for the shrill whistle of a teakettle or the weeping of a mysterious Squonk, he felt as if he was seeing Camp Pukwudgee for the first time. Most of his fellow Jackalopes were still asleep when Dooley crept from his bottom bunk, slipped on his flip-flops and tiptoed out the door. On his way to the boys' latrine just two cabins down, he replayed the scenes from the day before in his mind—seeing Jenny on the rock as he and his parents drove by and again outside the mess hall. Through Sama, Jenny had told Dooley she'd find him, but when?

On his way back to the cabin, Dooley was lost in his thoughts. He didn't notice a slight rustling near a trio of birch trees.

"Psssttt…"

"Who's there?" Dooley asked, spinning around.

"My name is Tristen."

"Where are you?" Dooley asked. "I can't see you."

"I'm hiding. Hang on."

Dooley watched as a girl just taller than him with long blond hair stepped out from behind one of the slender birch trees. It looked to him as if she were walking through a door. One minute she wasn't there and the next she was.

"Why were you hiding behind that tree?" asked Dooley. "Actually, *how* were you hiding behind that tree?"

"I'm a Skrito. I can camouflage myself to stay hidden, you know like a chameleon."

"Oh, cool. Well, I'm going back to my cabin." Dooley pointed in the direction of the Jackalope cabin.

"Hey, everyone's talking about the girl you saw. What's her name?"

"Jenny," Dooley offered, stopping to turn back around and face Tristen.

"Jenny—right. So I came out early to try to see her."

"You're a Visus, too? Did you see Jenny?"

"No," Tristen answered. "I'm not exactly a Visus… at least not yet. I just thought I might be able to at least feel her presence. But I *am* a Geminus."

"Oh, my zodiac sign is Aries," Dooley replied, a little confused.

Tristen rolled her eyes. "A *Geminus* not a Gemini. That means I have double powers. You really don't know much about this stuff, do you?"

"I've only known about my power since the beginning of the summer. I'm still learning all the rules." Dooley looked down at the roots of the tree Tristen was leaning against, trying to hide his mortification and break her penetrating gaze. Though the early morning was still cool, he could feel himself sweating through his t-shirt.

"Don't you want to know what my other power is?"

Dooley took a breath and met her eyes again. "Uh, sure. What is it?"

"I'm an Empath." Tristen took a tiny step closer to Dooley. He stepped backwards only to find he was wedged against a tree.

"Like Beryl, right?"

"No, Beryl is telepathic, sometimes we call her power a Telephone. She can talk to others using her mind, like a one-sided conversation. Not very useful really." Tristen took another step, slowly raising her right hand until her thumb rested in between Dooley's eyebrows and her four fingers spread across the top of his head. "I can slip right into someone else's thoughts. I can feel their feelings. Read their deepest secrets."

Dooley gulped. Tristen's fingers felt like ice on his skin. He sensed something inside of him, his heart or his lungs or his stomach, slowly dropping down to his toes.

Suddenly, the silence of the campground was broken by the blaring siren of Busby's air horn.

"Wake up, Campers!" Busby shouted into his megaphone. "It's another pleasingly picture-perfect Pukwudgee day!"

Dooley slipped out from under Tristen's hand and ran to his cabin without looking back at her. He wove his way through the din of noisy boys as they hastily dressed for breakfast and badgered those still trying to sleep.

"Cyrano," Dooley said as he grabbed his friend's arm and pulled him into a sitting position. "I've got to talk to you."

Cyrano yawned. Then he put on his glasses and looked at Dooley, sleepily. "What's up?"

"I just had a really weird conversation with Tristen," whispered Dooley.

"Oh, yeah. She's pretty intense."

"No kidding. She was trying to read my thoughts or something, like this." Dooley placed his thumb and fingers on Cyrano's head.

Cyrano bat his hand away. "Cut it out, Dooley."

"I'm serious! She was asking me all of these questions about Jenny and talking about being a Gemini…"

"Geminus," Cyrano corrected. "Tristen is obsessed with being the best at everything. She's won the Perfect Pukwudgee Participant plaque for eight years in a row, ever since her first year at camp. Clio almost beat her last year, and I thought Tristen was going to lose her mind. Just stay away from her, Dooley."

"Oh. Okay," Dooley sunk into his bed, feeling a little less anxious. He slipped off his flip-flops and started pulling on his socks.

"We better get in line for breakfast or there'll only be cereal left. I overslept one day last year and I had to eat a bowl of Fiber Nuggets. It was like eating twigs floating in warm milk. Let's go."

Seven

FISHBOWLS

Dooley and Cyrano filled their plates with the last of the scrambled eggs and sausage links before joining Leo at the Jackalope table. Leo was picking tiny, yellow blobs out of his hair.

"What happened to you?" Cyrano asked Leo.

"This is what I get for trying to be nice," Leo answered. "I walked over to talk to Beryl, you know, just being friendly, right? And your crazy sister magicked scrambled eggs on my head."

"That's mean even for Clio. What did you say?"

"I was telling Beryl 'Good Morning.' No big deal."

"I didn't know you knew sign language," replied Cyrano.

"Actually, I don't," admitted Leo. "I asked Tristen to help me."

"That was your first mistake," Dooley said. "She is scary crazy."

"Show me what you did." Cyrano instructed Leo.

Leo aimed his right pointer finger at them. Next, he pinched his thumb and pointer finger together, set them against his forehead, turned them downward, then touched them to his forehead again. Finally, Leo made a fist with one hand and placed his other hand on top with the thumb of his first hand poking out and wiggling slightly. Cyrano and Dooley looked on in amused confusion.

"Tristen said it meant, 'I wish you a good morning, my budding buttercup.'" Leo said, sadly.

"You've got to be kidding." Virgil Lee, the older camper Dooley had met the day before, was standing nearby watching Leo. Virgil took off his headphones and gracefully vaulted onto the table, sitting in between breakfast plates. "You just signed: 'You're a moron turtle.' That is seriously hilarious, dude. But hey, Leo, don't beat yourself up. Sign language can be pretty difficult to master. As the Russians say: '*Blizok lokotok, da ne ukusish.*'"

"Yeah, thanks, Virgil. That's really helpful."

"That means 'Your elbow is close, and yet you can't bite it.'"

"Okay…" Leo replied, ready for further explanation.

"Sometimes things are harder than they look." Virgil slid his headphones back in place and hopped down from the table. "Farewell, my brothers, or as the Xhosa people say: *Ukuhamba, ba zalwana.*" Virgil strode out the door and into the sunshine.

"You weren't kidding when you said to stay away from Tristen." Dooley said. "It looks like she's out to get everyone." Dooley went on to explain to Leo what had happened on his way back from the latrine.

"I wonder why she was trying to see Jenny, the Ghost Girl?" asked Leo.

"Tristen probably just wants to add Ghost Hunter to her list of accomplishments." Cyrano answered. "Dooley, do you think you'll see Jenny today?"

"I have no idea, but I hope so."

The boys joined a large group of campers assembled outside the mess hall. Counselor Busby stood at the base of the flagpole, his ever-present clipboard at the ready. The flag raised high above him snapped in the morning breeze. Two clear glass bowls sat on top of a closed picnic basket on the ground at his feet. Busby scanned the chatting crowd and made check marks on his papers.

"Gather 'round, Pukwudgeeans! We're nearing zero eight hundred hours, and there's lots to do today! It looks like we're missing a few of our Gumberoo boys. Oh well, I'm sure they'll show up."

"Oh no," Cyrano whispered.

"What's wrong?" Dooley asked.

"Just get ready," Cyrano said as he pinched his nose. "Things are about to get pretty smelly."

"Before I forget, let me remind you that there is no malicious spell-casting at Camp Pukwudgee." Busby looked directly at Clio who matched his gaze with an exaggeratedly innocent look. "In fact, all spells should be cast under the strict supervision of an adult."

"Now?" Dooley whispered, anticipating the smell Cyrano's nose had predicted.

"Not yet," Cyrano replied.

"I have two fishbowls here. One with fun activities—fencing, leather crafts, rock polishing—and one with chores. You *must* pick from each fishbowl." Busby patted his shirt pocket. "And I have a few special chores set aside for any lucky campers who might benefit from the character-building afforded by extra service opportunities."

Suddenly, Tosh and Tut came tumbling over each other as they rounded the corner at the back of the mess hall.

"Run!" They screamed as they streaked past the stunned group. "Skunk!"

Dooley looked past the boys and saw a very angry-looking skunk charging toward them. Seeing the group of helpless campers, the skunk turned around, pointed her tail in the air and sprayed them with all her might before calmly walking back to her den.

Eight

GO DUCKS!

Everyone—except Cyrano who had heeded his smelly prophecy and ran inside the mess hall before the skunk sprayed—went to the cabins to changes clothes, shower and bring their stinky shirts and shorts to the camp cooks to be washed. Then they stood in line outside the nurse's cabin to be misted with a combination of hydrogen peroxide, vinegar and dish soap. Once they were clean, most of them returned to the flagpole area to pick the day's activities and chores.

Only Tosh and Tut could be found already hard at work in the kitchen, scraping out the black grease that had accumulated below the giant griddle where the daily rations of bacon and sausage were cooked each morning. As he walked them to their first chore, Busby had promised them a day full of "extra special service opportunities" as payment for their reckless aggravation of the mama skunk by the trash cans. The cooks were pleased to have the boys' help as they lifted the half-ton range so that the floor could be easily swept and mopped underneath.

"I got canoeing for my activity and weeding the camp vegetable garden for my chore," said Dooley after he chose from the fishbowls. "What about you?"

"I'm on trash patrol." Cyrano held up a slip of paper displaying a cartoonish picture of a bug with a diagonal line crossing over it and the words:

SAY NO TO THE LITTER BUG

"And then I'm heading to the craft shack." Cyrano showed Dooley a different slip of paper with a picture of a dream catcher on it and the phrase:

IF YOU CAN DREAM IT, YOU CAN DO IT

"All right. Well, see ya later," Dooley said.

"Yeah, see ya," answered Cyrano.

After Dooley and a few other campers had pulled all of the weeds (and some of the smaller green bean plants they had thought were weeds) from the vegetable garden, they were released to their activities.

Once he had consulted a map pinned to the bulletin board in the mess hall, Dooley found the dock where six canoes of varying sizes were lined up and ready to be launched.

"Welcome campers," said a pear-shaped woman in a red swimsuit, black athletic shorts and flip-flops. "As most of you know, I am Penelope Canard, Coach Penny to those of you on the Camp Pukwudgee Swim Team—GO DUCKS!—and I'll be helping you get out in the canoes today. Before you board and practice some dry-land rowing techniques, notice the three vessel sizes. The red canoes will hold three paddlers. The silver canoes will hold two paddlers. And the blue canoes are solos—one paddler per boat."

Dooley scanned the group of fellow "paddlers" and noticed Tristen looking directly at him. Quickly he turned back around to face Coach Penny and listen to her instructions, a quiver of panic pulsing below his sternum.

"Everyone needs to suit up with a life jacket. Then choose your canoe. Find a partner or make a trio. Or for you more adventurous types, claim a solo canoe."

Dooley made a beeline for a blue canoe, but in his haste, he stumbled over a smaller camper wearing a hot pink backpack covered in gold foil stars who had bent over to tie her shoe.

"Hey, watch out!"

"Oh! Sorry."

"Dooley?" It was Celeste. Cyrano's younger sister.

"Oh, hey," Dooley replied as he backed slowly toward a solo canoe.

"Have you ever canoed before?" asked Celeste.

"Yeah, sort of. I used to ride those giant Swan Boats in the Public Garden lagoon when I lived in Boston."

Dooley noticed one of the solo canoes was already taken.

"I'm kinda nervous," Celeste whispered confidentially as she fiddled with the straps of her backpack. "I heard that they take the canoes way out and that Coach Penny will

throw you in the river if you say you can't swim and that
she has webbed feet like a duck and that she can hold her
breath underwater for an hour and…"

"Come on, Celeste," Dooley sighed. "It'll be okay." Dooley
grabbed her hand and led her to a silver canoe. "Be my
partner."

Nine

THE HACHE RIVER

Dooley extended his legs and flexed his calf muscles, balancing his paddle across his knees. After paddling in circles for the first few minutes, he and Celeste had finally found their rhythm, taking their canoe swiftly down the Hache River. Now an hour into their voyage, the river broadened and the current slowed. Slender birch trees grew along the banks, leaning sideways with leafy branches dipping into the water. Decaying logs floated near the bank, wedged in by a maze of algae-covered tree roots.

"Hey, Dooley," Celeste called from her seat at the front of the canoe without turning around to look at Dooley in the stern, "Did you hear Coach Penny say it's called the Hache River because *hache* means ax in French and the river is shaped like an ax?"

"Yep," answered Dooley, "Lumberjacks used The Hache to float logs to the Mississippi River." Dooley leaned back against the deck and looked up at the blue sky above the tree branches. He inhaled the slick, earthy smell of the river as he tried to imagine the lumberjacks from centuries past with their red plaid shirts and their suspenders and their giant saws and their blue oxen. Dooley realized he didn't know much about lumberjacks apart from Paul Bunyan.

"Dooley, look! We're coming to the ax-head!"

Dooley sat up and saw that the river made a sharp left up ahead. To the right, he noticed a crowding of weeping willow trees packed in a clump at the base of a stout hill. Water was spinning in a whirlpool below the low-hanging branches. Dooley could just make out a faint orange glow pulsing in the shadowy darkness made by the tangle of leaves.

"Let's paddle over there, Celeste, to the right."

"But we'll run into the bank. It's just a hill behind those trees."

"I want to see what's glowing back there."

"Glowing?" Celeste asked. "I don't see anything glowing."

The hairs stood up on Dooley's neck, and he felt a creeping up his scalp. They paddled mightily against the flow to veer to the right and found themselves spinning in the whirlpool.

"Grab a branch and pull us through," Dooley ordered. Celeste complied and Dooley grabbed one, too. Soon, they had slid under the trees and into a river cave.

They blinked their eyes and held their breath as they attempted to adjust to the darkness of the cave. "I can't see anything, Dooley. Can you?"

"Sort of," Dooley answered, "But mostly, it just looks

like glowing light." The dull glimmer reminded Dooley of burning ash at the end of a bonfire.

"Hang on," Celeste said as she rummaged through her backpack. "Maybe this will help."

Celeste pulled out a small battery-operated camping lantern. After switching it on, she shined it on the walls on either side of them, helping them realize that they had entered a narrow passageway. Dooley could touch the rough cave walls on both sides just by stretching out his arms. Surrounded by so much darkness, they could only see a few feet in each direction.

"Now what do you see, Dooley?" came a voice behind them.

Dooley and Celeste both spun around so quickly they nearly capsized their canoe. When the blue canoe reached them, Dooley saw the paddler's long blond hair appear gradually as she entered the circle of Celeste's lantern light.

"Tristen," said Dooley, gloomily.

"You don't sound very happy to see me," Tristen said, frowning. "And this must be the littlest Mulligan." Tristen's face was veiled in shadows that exaggerated the arch of her eyebrows and the length of her nose.

Celeste glanced at Tristen then turned to face forward again. "I'm Celeste," she gulped.

"And what's your power, sweetie?" Tristen asked, imitating a nurturing manner.

"I'm a Caelum."

"You like stars? That's just adorable. Well, I'm Tristen Bergman—Blue Class Empath and *Silver* Class Skrito—at your service."

Dooley noticed Celeste's discomfort. "A Skrito is a—"
He began to explain, sympathetically.

"She's a hider," interrupted Celeste as she folded her arms
across her chest. "I know, Dooley."

"Okay, so now that we've all been introduced, what do you
see, Dooley? Because, I can't see anything except gray stone."

Celeste handed Dooley the lantern, and he held it close
to the wall on his right. He squinted and cleared his throat.
"It looks kind of like paintings—cave paintings—I guess.
This is a picture of a sunflower," he said, pointing to a spot
on the wall. "And this is a shell, like a snail shell."

Celeste opened her back pack and pulled out a pen and
notebook with a picture of a kitten on the cover. "Sunflower.
Shell. What else, Dooley?" she asked while writing.

Their canoes continued to float further into the cave.
Dooley shined the lantern on the opposite wall. "Here's a
big pinecone."

Tristen sighed dramatically. "This is a waste of time. It's
just a bunch of drawings."

"Yes, but who made them? It would have to be a Visus.
They're made with special ink only visible to another Visus.
Which would explain why only I can see it."

They continued to float through the darkening cave as
Dooley flashed the light from one picture to the next. Suddenly, he shouted and dropped the lantern.

"Let's go! Celeste, turn around and start paddling!"

"Why?" Celeste asked as she fumbled with her paddle.
"What is it, Dooley?"

"I saw something."

"Another pinecone?" Tristen asked, sarcastically.

"No, not a pinecone. Something else with big teeth, and it… it smiled at me, so let's get out of here!"

Ten

LEONARDO FIBONACCI

"But what was it? What did you see?" Celeste asked for what seemed to Dooley the 100th time since they had paddled out of the cave.

"Celeste, I don't know." He was beginning to show his irritation at the persistency of this eight-year-old girl. "If I knew I would tell you."

"It was a creature? Not a painting?"

"It moved. It was real… I think." Dooley wasn't sure exactly what he saw, but he knew there were big eyes and white teeth and a kind of alarm went off inside his mind when he saw it, pressing him to leave immediately.

Tristen pulled her canoe on the shore, followed by Dooley and Celeste. He took off his life jacket and tossed it in the canoe with the paddles. Then without saying a word to Tristen, Dooley grabbed Celeste's hand and led her away.

"Where are we going, Dooley?" Celeste asked.

"We're going to find Counselor Busby. I've got to tell somebody what I saw."

Dooley asked several of the older campers fishing nearby where they could find Busby. They instructed him to go past the nurse's clinic, past the head counselor cabin, until they reached the edge of the Bloodstone Forest. They found him on his knees bending over a cluster of red-capped mushrooms with white spots covering their tops. He was muttering softly, "Who's a deadly mushroom? Not you! No, you're a pretty toadstool. Yes, you are! Prettiest in all the Fungi Kingdom."

"Um… Counselor Busby?" Dooley interrupted.

Busby stood up quickly and brushed off the pine needles and dirt from his knees and hands.

"Dooley! Celeste! I was just inspecting a beautiful troop of *Amanita muscaria,* otherwise known as fly agaric mushrooms. I'm the President of our local Mycological Society—that's a club for mushroom enthusiasts—and these are some of my favorites. Celeste, did your sister Calix tell you about them? She was always such an eager Greenie, not unlike myself!"

"No. We're here to tell you about something we saw on the Hache River," responded Dooley.

"Well, come sit on my porch. I always have time for Pukwudgee prodigies!"

Busby's porch was crowded with potted ferns and rocking

chairs. A lumpy dog bed sat at the eastern end where it could be shaded from the afternoon sun. Once they had situated themselves in the chairs, Busby asked, "Now what can I do for you clever campers?"

Dooley explained about the canoe ride and the glowing and the paintings.

"What kind of paintings did you see?" asked Busby.

Celeste took out her notebook and read off the names: "Sunflower, shell, pinecone…" And then in a whisper, "creepy beast."

"The shell—was it like a clam shell or a snail shell?"

"Uh, snail. It had a spiral shape," answered Dooley

"Fibonacci," Busby replied, nodding his head slightly.

"Bless you," said Celeste, thinking Busby had sneezed. "I hope you're not allergic to all these plants!"

"No, Fibonacci. All of those pictures you saw were of things in nature which represent the Fibonacci Sequence."

Busby stepped down from the porch to pick a purple flower from the assortment of tall wildflowers in the flower beds bordering the front of the cabin.

"The purple coneflower, scientific name: *Echinacea purpurea*," Busby said, adoringly. "This common wildflower holds a complicated mathematical principle right here." Busby pointed to the orange and brown seed head in the center. "Leonardo Fibonacci was a mathematician born in the 12th century. He realized that there was a recurring sequence of numbers found in nature, and you come up with this sequence when you add the preceding sums together."

Dooley and Celeste gave him a puzzled look.

"Starting with 0+1 which equals 1. Then 1+1=2. Then 1+2=3. 2+3=5. And so on. The sequence goes like this: 0, 1, 1, 2, 3, 5, 8, 13, 21, 34, 55, 89…"

"144," added Celeste.

"That's right!" Busby beamed.

"But what does that have to do with pinecones and snail shells?" Dooley asked.

"If you look at the seeds on this coneflower, you can count 13 spirals turning left and 21 spirals turning right," said Busby.

"Those are both numbers in the sequence," Celeste answered.

"You got it! When you look at the cross section of a nautilus shell like the one on a snail, you can see the size proportions measure similarly." Busby sat back contentedly in his chair. "It's really marvelous when you see how perfectly these things are designed. These seeds are arranged in the most compact and efficient way. No mathematician could design it any better."

"But why would someone—a Visus, I guess—draw pictures of things in nature with that sequence? Was it just a coincidence?" Dooley wondered.

"Tell him about that other… thing," Celeste prodded Dooley.

"I did see something else—a creature—in the cave, Counselor Busby, something that wasn't a drawing."

"Was it something you remember from our Camp Safety Seminar?" Busby asked.

"I'm not sure. I only saw it for a second, but it had sharp

teeth and these giant eyes. It was some kind of big, hairy monster."

"I don't know what to tell you about that, but I'll keep an eye out for any new creatures." Busby looked at his wristwatch. "It's time for you two to wash up for supper."

Dooley and Celeste walked down the porch steps to head to their separate latrines.

"Thank you for your help," said Dooley.

"Any time, kids!" Busby waved to them before quickly disappearing inside his cabin.

Eleven

SENSEI ELENORE

"**H**urry up, Dooley!" Cyrano called to his friend. "I'm starving!" While they were washing their hands, Dooley had pulled him aside to tell Cyrano about his afternoon adventures in the cave before Busby sounded the air horn for supper. Now the line of campers were filing in to the mess hall, but Dooley lingered outside, hoping to get another glimpse of Jenny.

Disappointed, Dooley eventually joined Cyrano in line just outside the mess hall door. "What's for supper?" Dooley asked.

Cyrano sniffed the air. "Fried chicken, mashed potatoes and corn. You know, you might be surprised but making crafts actually builds up an appetite. Which reminds me…" Cyrano pulled something out of his pants pocket and held it out for Dooley to see. "I made this for you."

"What is it?" Dooley asked, trying not to sound too baffled by Cyrano's creation as he looked at a mass of bright green yarn wrapped around a configuration of sticks and something like a small ball. The ball had two tiny black beads in the center, a line of red stitches near the bottom and a chrome chain and ring attached at the top.

"Duh. It's a keychain."

"Okay. I get that, but what is that? A voodoo doll?"

"No, it's not a voodoo doll," answered Cyrano, a bit offended. "It's a string doll and it's supposed to be you. Here are your eyes and mouth, and these are your arms and legs. Listen, if you don't want it…"

"I'll take it! I'll take it!" Dooley grabbed it from Cyrano's hand. "It just threw me off because it's, you know—green."

"Well, Sensei Elenore didn't have any yarn that actually looked like skin color, just greens and blues mostly."

"Why is the Crafts teacher called *sensei* anyway? Is she Japanese?" asked Dooley, happy to change the subject and hoping he hadn't hurt Cyrano's feelings.

"No. She's not Japanese, but she just really likes learning about new cultures and history. She's got this whole dojo thing going on at the craft shack this year. Last year, she made us call her Princess Elenore and everything was about castles and dragons and stuff. She's a Brush like Leo, and you know those arty types—always worked up over something!"

They filled their trays and walked toward the Jacka-lope table. Just as soon as they sat down, someone yelled, "Waddle-dee-wop! Sama's got the bloodstone!" The mess hall erupted in shouts.

"What's going on?" Dooley asked.

"There's this bloodstone, a rock that looks like it's covered in blood but it's really just dark green jasper with streaks of rust-red iron trapped inside it—my first year at camp the craft shack had this paleontologist theme and 'Elenore-saurus' taught us about rocks and fossils. Anyway, the bloodstone just shows up every once in a while. If you get it, you have to return the stone to this hole in a tamarack tree in the Bloodstone Forest."

All of the campers slapped the tables and stomped their feet with a steady beat. Then they chanted in unison:

Waddle-dee-wop! Ploddle-dee-plum!

Count to one and cut your thumb!

Waddle-dee-wop! Faddle-dee-foo!

Count to two and stir the brew!

Waddle-dee-wop! Beedle-dee-bee!

Count to three and skin your knee!

Waddle-dee-wop! Noodle-dee-nor!

Count to four and shout for more!

Waddle-dee-wop! Chiddle-dee-chive!

Count to five and come alive!

Sama stood up and squared her shoulders. Then she marched determinedly out the door and toward the dusky forest, gripping the smooth stone in her hand.

"When Sama gets to the tree, she has to find the hole and say the Waddle-dee-wop," explained Cyrano. "After she leaves the stone, she can come back."

"What happens if she doesn't leave the stone?" asked Dooley.

"Probably nothing, but there's a legend that the smell of a bloodstone attracts the Snallygaster."

"Snallygaster?"

"The giant one-eyed bird with scissor teeth that can swoop down and snatch you right up and…"

"Okay," said Dooley, "I got it. But I thought the Bloodstone Forest was too dangerous for us to go in?"

"Sama will be okay." Cyrano scooped up a spoonful of corn and chewed hungrily. "She's pretty tough and besides she's a Locito—you know, an Ear. She'll hear whatever's lurking around out there before she even sees it. And if she does hear something, she'll remember every word of it. She's an Ear with an elephant's memory."

Twelve

THE BLOODSTONE

Only a handful of campers remained inside the mess hall. Clio and Beryl waited patiently for Sama to return, glancing at the door every few minutes to see if she was back. The camp cooks were clanging pots and pans in the kitchen as they cleaned them in the deep metal sinks. One of the younger kitchen helpers with a colorful bandana tied around his head hummed softly, causing a rag to magically wipe down the countertops. Dooley and Cyrano were finishing their dessert of banana pudding and quietly discussing what Dooley saw at the back of the cave.

"Did the teeth look like tusks?" Cyrano asked. "Because it could've been a Gowrow."

"No. They weren't tusks," answered Dooley. "Just two rows of sharp white teeth."

"Could Celeste see it?"

Cyrano stacked their empty Styrofoam bowls, preparing to throw them away.

"I don't think so. But she was writing in her notebook so she may have been looking down. I just flashed the light on the creature for a second, and then I told her we needed to get out of there." Dooley and Cyrano stood up.

Sama entered the mess hall, stopping only a moment to sign to Beryl by holding both hands in front of her, palms facing in and wiggling her fingers. "Wait," said Sama as she passed the girls' table. Then she approached Dooley.

"I heard her again," she said. "Jenny spoke to me in the forest."

"What did she say?" Dooley asked.

"I was trying to find the tree with the hole—most of the trees look the same in there—and I was starting to get nervous. I kept walking deeper into the forest. It was getting dark and there were sounds; soft, scratching, shushing sounds, and they were coming from all around me. Then I heard a voice. It said, 'Not that one. Keep going.'"

Clio and Beryl had joined them, and Clio was signing to Beryl as Sama spoke.

"Then what happened?" asked Cyrano.

"I said, 'Jenny, is that you?' And she said, 'Yes. Seek out the tree with the blushing pinecones.' So I kept walking until I heard water rushing so I knew the Hache River was close. Then I saw this really tall tree with light green pine needles and pink pinecones. There were a bunch of holly bushes around it so it was hard to get close, but I found the hole and stuck the bloodstone in it."

"Did Ghost Girl Jenny say anything more?" Clio asked. "Or was she gone after you completed your chore?"

"I called to her, and she was quiet for a few minutes. Then she told me she had to leave."

"She seems scared," Dooley said, mostly to himself.

Sama nodded in agreement. "I asked her if she was afraid of something, if she was in danger from some creature or person. She said, 'Cowards die many times before their deaths; the valiant never taste of death but once.'"

"Shakespeare," responded Cyrano. "That's from *Julius Caesar*."

Clio smiled at her brother. "Cyrano, I'm wowed. Mom would be proud!"

"Yeah, that's not all." Sama closed her eyes to remember more. "Then Jenny said, 'Hope is the thing with feathers that perches in the soul and sings the tune without the words and never stops at all.' That's Emily Dickinson."

"So we know she likes to quote famous literature, but we still don't know what her deal is," Cyrano said. "Like why is she haunting Camp Pukwudgee?"

"I have no idea," said Sama. "After the Dickinson quote, she was gone or at least silent."

Beryl tapped Sama's shoulder and signed to her.

"Maybe. It's worth a try," Sama said to Beryl, before turning to address Dooley. "Beryl says you need to check out the Pukwudgee Historical Society. She thinks the answer to Jenny's present problems may lie in the past."

"Okay. I didn't know there was a historical society," said Dooley. "Where is it?"

"It's not really a historical society," Cyrano said. "It's more like a room with a bookshelf full of scrapbooks about the camp."

"All campers to your cabins," Busby called through the megaphone from outside the mess hall. "Lights out in 30 minutes."

"It's at the back of the craft shack," continued Cyrano. "I'll take you there in the morning."

TUESDAY

CRAFT DOJO

Before breakfast, Dooley and Cyrano headed to the craft shack to browse the Camp Pukwudgee scrapbooks. Once there, Dooley had his first good look at the building—a red, pagoda-like structure with four tiered-roof eaves and sliding rice paper doors. There was a large, open area in front which was covered by a white metal roof. Six splatter-painted picnic tables filled the open area. A banner with Japanese symbols hung from each column holding up the metal roof.

"I think Sensei Elenore is going to get out the wood burning kits today," said Cyrano as he sniffed the air. "I wish I could pick the craft shack again for my activity."

"Wow," Dooley said, "you weren't kidding about the dojo theme. Does she have to rebuild the craft shack every year?"

"Sort of, but it's part of her power to create big art. Pretty cool, huh?" Cyrano smiled. "In the years I've been to camp it's been a medieval castle, a pirate ship, a giant tree, a brontosaurus…"

Elenore slid open a door and stepped into her sandals just outside. She was wearing full black pants, a billowing white shirt and a wide belt of black fabric tied around her waist and knotted at the side. Her silver hair was twisted into a loose bun on the top of her head, and an indigo blue scarf covered most of her forehead. A pair of reading glasses hung from a multi-colored beaded chain. She bowed when she saw the boys and said, "Konnichiwa!"

"Good morning, Sensei Elenore," Cyrano replied. "This is my friend Dooley."

"Welcome to my craft dojo!" said Elenore. "It's a pleasure to meet you. But aren't you boys a little early for activity time?"

"We've come to look at the Pukwudgee Historical Society," answered Dooley.

"I applaud your enthusiasm." Elenore patted Dooley on the back heartily. "Camp Pukwudgee has quite a story to tell. I have to get my supplies ready for today, but you boys can help yourself to the scrapbooks in the back."

"Thank you… uh, *domo arigatou*," said Cyrano as he bowed self-consciously. The boys removed their shoes and slid open the door.

"Sayōnara!" Elenore called to them.

Once inside, Cyrano led the way past a kitchen with a pottery oven and a table covered with a crumbling mound of gray clay, past a room with floor-to-ceiling windows on two walls and a dozen canvases on easels positioned by a dozen stools, past a store room with storage cabinets crammed full of art supplies, and past a small bathroom. The last room was a mud room, originally intended for people to come in the back door and shed their dirty shoes and wet coats. It had a brick floor, and brick walls with a row of hooks by the door. A simple braided rug covered most of the floor and there were two rocking chairs with matching footstools. On the left, there was a sooty wood-burning stove and the wall was covered with framed photographs of varying sizes. Against the wall to the right was a tall bookshelf lined entirely with identical dark blue books. On the spine of each book was a year, beginning at the top with 1945.

"I didn't know Camp Pukwudgee has been around this long," Dooley exclaimed as he looked at the rows of books. "How are we going to get through all of these?"

"Let's split it up. I'll start at the beginning, 1945; and you start with 1960," Cyrano stood on a footstool and took down two books. "We'll just keep going until we see something that might be about Jenny."

He handed Dooley a scrapbook and said, "Hold on." Cyrano stepped out of the room and returned with drawing paper and pencils from the store room. "Now, let's get started."

Fourteen

PUKWUDGEE HISTORICAL SOCIETY

Dooley was deep into his eighth scrapbook and still in the 1960s. He saw a picture of a teenaged girl wearing a tie-dyed t-shirt and wide-legged jeans. She was holding a paint brush and standing by a giant peace sign painted on the side of a cabin. Dooley could've sworn the girl was a young Sensei Elenore. Just as he was about to show the picture to Cyrano, his stomach growled loudly. "What time is it?" he asked.

Cyrano looked at his watch. "Uh-oh, it's 9:30. We've already missed breakfast and flagpole announcements."

The boys' scribbled notes about Camp Pukwudgee were scattered around them. As Dooley gathered the papers and Cyrano reshelved the scrapbooks, they discussed their findings.

"So they started Camp Pukwudgee in an old, abandoned logging camp in 1940 but they didn't start making scrapbooks until 1945," said Cyrano. "And from what I can tell, at first they mainly wanted to hide kids like us so the government wouldn't try to use their powers to win wars and stuff."

"How could a bunch of kids do anything to help an army, anyway?" Dooley asked.

"I guess they could read an enemy general's mind or carve beasts that come to life or translate coded messages. Or maybe even predict if a bomb were going to drop by the smell the of it." Cyrano said proudly as he brushed the dust off his hands.

"That's true." Dooley glanced at the framed pictures on the wall. "I just wish we could've found something about Jenny. I never saw her picture or her name or anything."

"Yeah, I looked for the name Jenny on every page." Cyrano hopped down from a footstool. "We better go get our activities and chores from the fishbowls. And maybe they'll have something left over from breakfast. I'm so hungry I could eat a Squonk right now, warts and all."

"Cyrano, look at this!" Dooley exclaimed, excitedly.

Cyrano stood by his friend to study the pictures. There were a few old-fashioned looking portraits, but most were framed newspaper clippings. One was from the *Minneapolis Tribune* and showed a grainy, black and white photograph of a line of men holding pickaxes and saws. The men were flanked by trees tall enough that their tops weren't included in the picture and a modest, wooden shack with a smoking chimney behind them. The caption read: *October 9, 1904 – Typical Logging Camp, Showing Cook and Sleeping Shanties.*

"What is it?" Cyrano asked.

Dooley pointed to a different newspaper clipping. There was a woman standing in a large kitchen with her hands on her hips and a dish towel tied around her waist to protect her long dress. She looked annoyed, as if she had a lot of work to do and didn't want to stop for a photograph. Two small boys stood in front of a pile of firewood on one side of the woman. They both wore overalls, and the older boy had a polka-dot bandana tied around his neck. A girl stood on the other side, her hand reaching into a barrel of potatoes. The girl wore a white pinafore apron.

Dooley squinted to see what was stitched on the pocket, but it was too blurry. He read the caption aloud, "Logging Camp Cook Carrie Johansson with her children Caleb, Peter, and Jenny."

"Jenny? So is that her?" Cyrano whispered. He took off his glasses and cleaned them of the dust from the old books before replacing them on his long nose.

"I think that's the girl I saw, but she looks younger in this picture."

They scanned the rest of the framed photographs, looking for more of Jenny. They finally spotted a portrait of three glum-faced people—a woman, a girl and a little boy. The woman and the girl sat stiffly on wooden chairs. The little boy sat in the woman's lap and a large Golden Retriever sprawled at their feet, the girl's fingers resting lightly on the dog's back. Dooley glanced back and forth between the photograph and the newspaper clipping. "Okay, so this looks like Jenny and her mom Carrie and maybe one of the brothers," he said. "Jenny looks a little older in this one—more like how I've seen her around camp."

"I wonder what happened to her," said Cyrano, still whispering. "Like how she—died?"

"I don't know." Dooley rubbed the back of his neck. He had the same creepy feeling he had felt inside the cave the day before.

"Check out the dog, Dooley," said Cyrano.

"What do you mean?" Dooley asked.

"It looks like it's wearing the brother's bandana from the newspaper picture."

Dooley leaned in to examine the photograph more carefully.

"Boys!" Elenore entered the room suddenly, startling Dooley and Cyrano. "I assumed you'd left hours ago. Head Counselor Busby will not be pleased with your tardiness! Off to your chores and activities!" she warbled, smiling and hurrying them out the back door. "There's so much to do!"

Fifteen

TUESDAY ACTIVITIES

ooley and Cyrano ducked into the mess hall to beg for something to eat. They left mostly disappointed with two overly ripe bananas and a burnt waffle to share. "I can't believe we missed Waffle Day," Cyrano said, sadly. "They put chocolate chips in some of them and squirt whipped cream on top."

At the flagpole, they only found a disgruntled head counselor clutching his clipboard, irritably. "Boys, this is unacceptable. Where have you been?" Busby asked.

The boys explained about the their quest to learn about Camp Pukwudgee and how they lost track of time in the craft shack. Busby's face brightened slightly.

"Well, I do like to see my campers show plenty of Pukwudgee pride." Busby took a deep breath and continued more cheerfully. "Cyrano, choose from the bowls. Dooley, Tristen informed me that you asked her to draw your chore and activity, so I suggest you find her and get your day started."

Dooley gave Cyrano a pleading look before Busby said, "Let's go, boys. The thrills of Camp Pukwudgee wait for no boy or beast!"

Cyrano chose papers from the two fishbowls, and the boys began to walk toward the cabins. "I have toilet-scrubbing for my chore and bird-watching for my activity. This day is going to be great," said Cyrano, sarcastically.

"Let's hurry and finish our activities so we can get back to searching for more information about Jenny," said Dooley. "Besides, I'd rather scrub all the toilets at camp instead of hanging out with Tristen the Terrible. She gives me the willies."

Suddenly, Tristen appeared in front of them, popping up from behind a row of hedges on the edge of their path. "That's not very nice, Dooley."

The boys jumped back in alarm. "Tristen," Dooley yelped, "do you have to do that?"

"Do what?" Tristen asked.

"Jump out like that!" Dooley answered. "It's annoying."

"Sorry, Dooley but I've been waiting for you for over an hour," replied Tristen. "I wanted to give you this." Tristen held out a scrap of paper with a picture of a canoe printed in the center. "We're heading back to the cave."

"You're not supposed to draw the same activity twice in a row," said Cyrano. "That's against Busby's rules."

"What are you, the Camp Police? Well, thanks for the info, Officer Cyra-Nosey," Tristen snapped at Cyrano, "but Dooley and I have important things to do. Why don't you go clean a toilet?"

Dooley watched Cyrano stomp off toward the boys' latrine, wishing he could stay with his friend.

"So how *did* you get us canoeing for our activity again?" asked Dooley.

"Simple. I found out who drew it and switched with them." Tristen repositioned the drawstring bag on her shoulder and began walking toward the dock. "Tosh and Tut Nelson are the most gullible campers ever. I told them that Smitty, the Lake Monster, spent every Tuesday morning in the Hache River. They nearly begged me to take these from them."

"You're really frightening, Tristen," said Dooley as he tried to keep up with Tristen's long legs.

Tristen sighed and rolled her eyes. "I'm not trying to scare anyone. I'm just motivated. I want to be the best at everything."

"You know that's not possible, right? You can't be the best at everything."

"Well, not with that attitude. Now let's get to the dock and explore that cave again. There's got to be more to it than just stupid pictures of sunflowers."

Sixteen

BACK TO THE CAVE

One silver canoe remained on the shore when Dooley and Tristen arrived. Coach Penny and all the other campers were already out. They strapped on their life vests, put the canoe in and began to paddle down the river with Tristen in front and Dooley in the stern.

In the cave, Tristen opened her bag and pulled out a large yellow flashlight. She switched it on, spreading a wide, bright shaft of light across the cave walls.

"That's much brighter than Celeste's lantern," said Dooley as he gazed at the walls. "I can see a lot more now."

"And she calls herself a Caelum. What kind of 'Star-Stopper' can't even light up a dark room?" Tristen said, snidely.

"Well, she literally stopped time, so let's see you try that," Dooley muttered under his breath.

"What was that, Dooley?" said Tristen, as she turned around and directed her high-powered flashlight right into Dooley's eyes.

"Nothing," Dooley responded, shielding his eyes. "Do you mind?"

"Oh, forgive me," she smiled. "Is the light bothering you?"

Tristen continued to illuminate the walls on either side of them as they floated down the length of the cave.

"Here's the spot where I saw the creature," Dooley said. "Just up ahead."

A ledge jutted out of the cave wall to the right. Tristen shined her light on something resting on the ledge—a shapeless, grayish bulk. "It looks like a pillow or a sofa cushion," she said.

As they passed the object, Dooley hesitantly reached his hand out to touch it then pulled his hand back quickly. He noticed his palm was covered with coarse, pale hair. He wiped his hand on his shirt as they continued to float deeper into the cave than they had the day before. Moments later, they floated through a curved opening and into a larger room.

"Do you see anything different in here, Dooley?" Tristen asked, her voice bouncing and echoing in the wider space.

"Same things: paintings of pinecones and snail shells and sunflowers. Did you know that those are all examples of the Fibonacci Sequence?" asked Dooley, proudly. "You use this math formula—the numbers get bigger because you add the last two together and..."

"Duh," Tristen interrupted him. "Everyone knows about that."

"Oh, I'd never heard about it until Busby explained it to me. But I still don't know what it has to do with..." Dooley stopped talking and stared at a spot near the top of the wall. "Tristen, shine the light over there."

"What is it?"

"It's says something… the word: HOPE, with a spiral in the *O*."

"Big deal," she groaned.

"Under that it says: 'If it were not for hope, the heart would break. Build hopefulness adding a little more to what you had the day before.'"

"Isn't that just the sweetest? Maybe you could write that down in a card and send it to your grandma for her birthday," Tristen said, mockingly. "This is so frustrating! What good is a cave with hidden paintings and messages if it doesn't lead you to a treasure or solve a hundred-year-old mystery. This is lame. Let's go back."

Tristen started to turn around to paddle back out of the cave, but Dooley grabbed the flashlight from her and shined it on the other wall. "Do you have a pen and paper?" he asked.

"Yes. I've got some in my…"

"Okay," Dooley interrupted. "Write this down."

Seventeen

HOPE'S DAUGHTERS

"**R**ead it back to me so I can make sure we got everything," said Dooley.

Tristen read from her notebook:

There once was a woman named was Hope. Though it was a strange name for that time, Hope loved its uniqueness and chose to give her daughters strange names, too. Her older daughter was born on a day full of thunder and lightning and hailstones. Hope named this tiny, black-eyed child Anger. Her second daughter was born the next year on a ghostly, moonless night. Hope named this strong, golden-haired child Courage. Anger fulfilled her namesake as she raged and exploded all the days of her childhood. But Hope patiently taught Anger to release her fury only when it was required—to help the helpless and protect the weak. Courage was wild and showed no fear, which often resulted in needless injuries. Hope taught Courage to how to judge when to act and when to be still. These daughters needed their mother as much as Hope needed them, for it is said, "Hope has two beautiful daughters; their names are Anger and Courage. Anger at the way things are, and Courage to see that they do not remain as they are."

"That's it," said Dooley. "You got it all." Dooley slumped down in his seat and rubbed his bleary eyes, exhausted from focusing on the long passage so painstakingly painted on the wall of the cave with magic ink.

"What reason would a Visus have to write all of this on a wall, especially since there's a good chance no one would ever see it?" asked Tristen. "It just doesn't make any sense."

"I have no idea. This just gets weirder and weirder." Dooley scanned the rest of the walls, looking for anything else he might have missed. Then, he shined the light on the ceiling. "Um… Tristen, let's turn around," he whispered.

"Great! Let's get out of here," she exclaimed.

"Shh!"

"Don't shush me, Dooley," Tristen said, loudly.

"Tristen, look up."

Tristen looked where Dooley was shining the flashlight. High above them, covering the entire expanse of the cave ceiling, were hundreds of shifting and flapping and twitching brownish-black blobs of fur and wings.

"Are those bats?" she whispered.

"Yes."

They paddled on one side to turn around and started moving towards the arched opening to return to the narrow passageway.

Suddenly, they heard a low snarl, followed by a silence-piercing howl. The sounds of flapping above them grew, and Dooley sensed a change in the air. "Paddle now!" he yelled.

Dooley dropped the flashlight in between the floorboards at his feet and paddled furiously. Their canoe bumped into a wall but eventually made it through the opening, in spite of the darkness. Dooley felt something whoosh past his ear, then several more. Soon there were bats soaring out of the cave, just inches above their heads.

Tristen and Dooley ducked down, making it difficult to paddle their way out. Unexpectedly, their canoe pitched down and lifted up, as if something heavy had fallen in the center of the boat. With no other aim than to exit the cave as quickly as possible, they continued paddling until they reached the willow branches at the entrance. Just as they passed through leaving the darkness of the cave, Dooley felt something warm and wet on his cheek. Lifting his head from its crouching posture, he looked up and locked eyes with a shaggy face. It had big brown eyes, a black nose, yellow fur and was panting enthusiastically, showing a bottom row of sharp, white teeth. As it licked him again, Dooley exclaimed in disbelief, "It's a dog, and it's wearing a polka dot bandana."

Eighteen

CYPRIPEDIUM REGINAE

Tristen spun around to look behind her. "Where did that dog come from?"

"I guess it was in the cave," he responded, wiping his cheek and nervously leaning away from the hulking mass sitting between them.

"Well, get it out!" she screamed.

"I'm not going to shove it into the river. What if it drowns? Paddle over to the side, and I'll push it onto the bank."

They paddled to the left until the canoe bumped into a muddy jumble of tree roots. Dooley tried to push the dog from behind with no luck. The dog wouldn't budge. Then Dooley jumped out, nearly slipping in the wet mud. Once he was standing in the drier grass, he patted both legs and called to the dog, "Here, doggy-doggy. Come here, boy." The dog hopped out and playfully tackled Dooley to the ground.

As soon as the dog had left the canoe, Tristen began to paddle away. "Wait! Tristen, wait for me!" Dooley called.

"No way! I'm allergic to dogs!" she said and then sneezed five times in a row. "And that one is completely disgusting!"

Dooley stood, patting the yellow dog's head as he watched her float away down the Hache River. "It looks like we're walking back, buddy," he told the dog. The dog barked once in response.

Dooley and the dog walked along quietly, following the curve of the river. Dooley was lost in his thoughts, wondering about all he had read on the cave wall and what it might mean. It felt good to stay in the shade of the trees. This coolness, along with the soft splashing of the river and his busy thoughts, made Dooley forget about the dog happily trotting alongside him. So when the dog suddenly sprinted away from him, Dooley had to shake himself awake before running after it.

When Dooley caught up with the dog, he found the animal curled up next to Counselor Busby with its head resting on its paws. Busby's left hand was petting the dog, and his right hand was drawing in a sketch book. Dooley arrived on the scene out of breath.

"Ah, Dooley!" said Busby. "I'm glad you're here. Just take a look at this beauty! *Cypripedium reginae, reginae* meaning queenlike. It's commonly known as the Showy Lady's Slipper. It's the state flower of Minnesota and no wonder! Have you ever seen anything so glorious?"

Dooley bent down to see what Busby was sketching. He had to admit that it actually was a very pretty flower— snowy white petals sitting on a hot pink pouch that looked just like a ballet slipper. "Yeah, it's really awesome," he answered, still breathing hard. "Counselor Busby…" Dooley began.

"It's a rare flower, too," Busby continued. "In unusual circumstances it takes as many as sixteen years to bloom, though five years isn't uncommon. Imagine waiting around for years and years as just an ordinary green shoot but with the potential of becoming this?"

"Uh-huh… yeah… cool. Is that your dog?"

"Who, this mangy fellow?" The dog rolled over so Busby could scratch his belly. "This old dog doesn't belong to anyone. He's the camp dog, I suppose." Busby found a stick and threw it up the embankment, away from the river. The dog took off to retrieve it. "He's been here ever since I've been a counselor, and the Head Counselor before me introduced me to him."

"How long have you been here?" asked Dooley.

"This is my tenth year as Head Counselor at Camp Pukwudgee," Busby said, proudly. "I was a regular counselor a few summers before."

"Were you ever a camper?"

"No, I didn't grow up in this area, so I never attended Pukwudgee as a camper." Busby slumped his shoulders, as if admitting this fact revealed a terrible personal flaw. "But I am proud to say that my great-grandfather was the man who started this camp."

"Really? That's pretty cool," answered Dooley, genuinely.

"Yes, it's quite an honor. My grandmother told me about the camp when I was a teen—her father was the one who opened Pukwudgee back in 1940—and I was determined to come back and be a part of it. I just wish I could've known him, my great grandfather. Peter Johansson was his name. He was only a part of the camp for a few years, then he moved away." The dog had returned with the stick and was waiting expectantly for Busby to pick it up and throw it again.

"Peter? Peter Johansson?" Dooley asked, thinking of the newspaper clipping he and Cyrano had seen in the Pukwudgee Historical society.

"That's right. I suppose Great-Grandfather looked at what was a worn down logging camp and saw its potential, just like the Lady's Slipper blooming into something amazing." Busby flipped his sketchbook closed. "Time for me to head back to my cabin, and I'd bet my last Hodag spike that you haven't done your chore yet." Busby smiled. Then he whistled to the dog and called, "Come on, Caleb. Come on, boy!"

Dooley watched the Head Counselor and Caleb the dog stroll toward Busby's cabin.

Nineteen

CALEB THE DOG

Dooley stood motionless, breathing heavily but not because of exhaustion. He felt rooted to the grassy spot where he stood. His muscles were tense. Something important seemed to be hidden just below the surface. After silently watching Busby and the dog walk past the nurse's clinic and out of sight, Dooley remembered he didn't have a chore assignment.

"Counselor Busby, wait a minute!" he called as he ran to catch up. Rounding the corner, he called again. "Counselor Busby!" Busby and Caleb stopped and turned around to face him.

"Yes? What is it, Dooley?" Busby asked.

"Tristen only gave me an activity and not a chore, so I was wondering…" Dooley looked around frantically, then noticed the tall weed-like plants growing along the back of Busby's cabin. "I was wondering if I could weed that area right there for you?"

"Those aren't weeds," Busby replied, "Those are medicinal herbs: wild rosemary for muscle pain and chamomile for insomnia and marigold for sore throats. But you can harvest my crop of *Taraxacum*, commonly known as dandelions."

"So, pull out the dandelions? I can do that."

"Alright. I'll get a bowl for you to collect the whole plant. I use the roots for my coffee, the leaves in my salad and I deep-fry the flowers in butter. Just delicious!"

Busby popped inside the cabin and came back with a wide, wooden bowl.

"Would it be alright if the dog—Caleb—stayed out here with me?" Dooley asked. "I always wanted a dog."

Busby smoothed down his moustache ponderingly. "Caleb will do what he wants, I expect. But I'll give you a little advice," Busby reached into his pocket and pulled out a package of peanut butter crackers. "If you give him a few of these, he'll be your friend forever." Busby handed the package to Dooley and went inside his cabin.

Dooley sat down next to the patch of yellow dandelions. He pulled open the plastic package and took out a round cracker. "Here, boy. I've got something for you."

Caleb took a few steps toward the cracker, sniffing hungrily. Dooley set the treat next to him on the ground, and Caleb lunged at it, devouring it in one bite.

Dooley stroked Caleb's broad, shaggy back. "Good dog. Want another one?"

"Woof. Woof." Caleb barked. Dooley set another cracker on the ground which Caleb answered with a short, "Yip."

"That's a polite dog," said a voice behind him. Dooley

turned to see Virgil Lee heading toward them, carrying a fishing pole and tackle box.

"What do you mean?" asked Dooley.

"Being a Vox, I've conquered most human languages at this point. I needed a new challenge, you know? So I worked all last semester exploring animal languages." Virgil set his fishing equipment on the ground and sat on the tackle box. "I went out in the field, learning prairie dog chirps and whale whistles. Fascinating work."

"Can you understand what any animal is saying?" asked Dooley.

"I prefer to study sophisticated creatures—much more interesting conversations. Take these cicadas, for instance." Virgil paused to listen to the high-pitched whine of the cicadas. Their song moved up and down, loud and soft. "It's just a bunch of boy cicadas saying, 'I am here' over and over. So boring."

"What about this dog? Could you understand him?"

"When I was walking up, I heard him say, 'Yes, please,' and then he said, 'Thanks.' It's highly unusual for animals to display what we'd consider good manners. Animals tend to be more straight forward with their language. 'Food good' or 'Me scared' is what you usually hear. Although there was this one extra chatty prairie dog who was obsessed with describing what everyone was wearing. One day, he actually made fun of my outfit, saying I shouldn't mix plaid and stripes."

Virgil yawned and rolled his shoulders. "It's time for a little siesta before supper," he said as he slowly rose to his feet. "Adiós, amigo."

"Hang on," said Dooley. "I need you to help me talk to this dog—to Caleb."

Twenty

BARK RUFF GROWL

"**O**kay," said Virgil, barely trying to hide the annoyance from his voice. He sat back down. "What do you want to say to the dog?"

"Um… I want to ask him…" Dooley wasn't sure what to ask first. He had so many theories and ideas rolling around his head. Then he took a deep breath, held the dog's face in his hands and looked him in the eyes. Calmly and directly Dooley asked Caleb, "Who are you?"

"Ru-ruff," barked Caleb.

"What did he say?" Dooley asked, excitedly.

"He said he wants another cracker," Virgil responded.

"Like he won't answer any of my questions unless I give him more crackers?"

"No. I don't think he understands your question. Just like you can't understand dog, he can't understand human. He just wants a cracker."

Dooley gave Caleb another cracker and sat back on his heels.

Virgil shook his head. "I'm surrounded by amateurs. Let me try. I picked up a bit of dog lingo last month." He got down on his hands and knees in a dog-like stance. "Golden Retrievers were originally bred in Scotland, so I'll try a Scottish accent." Virgil let out a confident bark.

Caleb imitated Virgil's stance and responded with a series barks and yips.

The expression on Virgil's face changed from uninterested to unbelief. He barked a few more times and Caleb yapped sadly before dropping back down and laying his chin on his paws.

"Wow," said Virgil.

"What is it? What did he say?" asked Dooley.

"Um, I think I'm getting this right…" Virgil paused to think and bit his lip. For the first time since Dooley had met him, this cool older camper seemed to drop his intimidating self-confidence. "Caleb just told me that he used to be a boy—a human boy. He had the power to change himself into animals and something went wrong. Now he's stuck in this body and has been for a very long time."

"Ask him about Jenny," said Dooley. "His sister."

Virgil looked confused but didn't ask Dooley what he meant. He barked his question and Caleb responded with a growl.

"He said this is all Jenny's fault," said Virgil, "and he doesn't want to talk about her."

"But why?" asked Dooley. "Ask him why it's her fault? What happened?"

Virgil barked again. This time, Caleb snarled angrily,

showing his teeth. Then he lunged toward Dooley, grabbed the package of crackers from his hand and ran away, galloping into the shadows of the Bloodstone Forest.

Virgil stood up and brushed off his hands. He calmly picked up his pole and tackle box.

"Well? What else did he say?" Dooley asked.

"He said that Peter lied. There is no hope."

WEDNESDAY

Twenty-One

PETER LIED

The next morning when they were getting ready in the cabin, Dooley noticed Cyrano and Leo giving each other wordless looks of concern. He knew those looks were about him, but he had needed the night to consider all he had learned about the Johansson family. He just hadn't been ready to talk yet. Now that he saw Cyrano's worried face, Dooley knew it was time to tell his friends about Caleb.

"Stop looking at me like that," said Dooley.

"Like what?" Cyrano asked.

"Like you think I'm nuts or something."

"Well, you haven't said a word since yesterday afternoon," Leo replied.

"Fine. I'll tell you what happened." Dooley looked around the room, noticing a couple of boys joking at the front of the cabin. He watched as the last two campers left and the cabin door swung shut behind them. Then Dooley grabbed his friends' arms and made them sit on either side of him on his bottom bunk.

"So there's this dog that runs around camp, right?" Dooley began.

"Caleb, the Golden Retriever?" Cyrano asked.

"Right. It turns out that he was the creature I saw in the cave. When I went back yesterday with Tristen, he scared a bunch of bats, and then he jumped in our canoe."

"I heard Tristen telling the nurse that she's allergic to dogs," said Leo. "She was covered in hives. I know it's wrong, but I was kind of happy that she was so miserable. I just couldn't help myself."

"I know," Dooley agreed. "But I am glad she made me go back to the cave because I might never have known who that dog really is."

"What do you mean?" asked Cyrano. "It's just an old dog."

"No. That's what I need to tell you. It's not just an old dog. It's a human trapped in a dog's body, a human named Caleb."

"How do you know that?" Cyrano asked.

"Virgil can translate dog language. He told me what Caleb was saying, or barking, or whatever. And here's the craziest part…"

"Crazier than a talking dog?" asked Leo.

"Yes." Dooley inhaled deeply. "Caleb was Jenny's brother."

"Jenny, the Ghost Girl?" Leo exclaimed.

"Wait," said Cyrano, "Jenny and Caleb and… what was the name of the other brother?"

"Peter," answered Dooley. "Peter started this camp, and he was Busby's great-grandfather."

"I don't remember reading anything in the scrapbooks about Peter," said Cyrano.

"The first scrapbook was from 1945, but the camp started in 1940," Dooley explained. "Busby said his great-grandfather only stayed around for a couple of years, and then he moved away. I guess he was gone by 1945."

"So this is all interesting, but it doesn't answer your questions about Ghost Girl," said Leo. "You still don't know how she died or why she's hanging around here or what she's scared of."

"Yeah, but it does make me wonder something else," said Dooley.

"What's that?" Cyrano asked.

"Well, we know where Caleb is, and we know where Jenny is." Dooley ducked out of the bunk and stood to face his friends. "But now we have a new question—what happened to Peter?"

"Do you think that's important? I mean, you said Busby told you he moved away," said Cyrano.

"The last thing Caleb said before he ran off was that Peter lied. Now, we need to find out what he lied about. As far as I can tell, there are probably only two people who know the answer," said Dooley.

"And by two people you mean a ghost and a dog, right?" Leo asked.

"Right."

Twenty-Two

SHAPE SHIFTING

After breakfast, the boys gathered with their fellow campers at the flagpole to receive their daily assignments. Instead of Counselor Busby supervising the morning meeting wearing his trademark red polo shirt and crisply-ironed khaki shorts, Sensei Elenore held the clipboard. She wore black leggings, black ballet slippers, and a t-shirt with a portrait of the artist Vincent Van Gogh. Over all of this, she wore a long, silk kimono adorned with pastel flowers. Elenore rolled up her wide sleeves, adjusted the reading glasses she kept on a beaded chain around her neck and began to check off the names of campers as they approached.

Once she was satisfied all of the campers were present, Elenore spoke. "Good morning, my cabbage dumplings! Head Counselor Busby had to drive in to town this morning, so he asked me to fill in for him. He wanted me to remind you that you cannot choose the same activity two days in a row." Cyrano shot a wide-eyed look at Tristen as if to say,

I told you! Tristen responded with an eye roll. "As always you will select your chore and your activity from these two fishbowls." Elenore took the fishbowls out of a large picnic basket and set them on the ground. "Choose and go forth to make your mark on the world, Pukwudgeeans!"

The campers lined up and drew the slips of paper from the bowls. Dooley stayed at the back of the line, with Leo and Cyrano in front of him. "I'm going to talk to Sensei Elenore to see if she knows anything about Jenny and her brothers," he told them.

After they had drawn out of the fishbowls, Cyrano and Leo showed Dooley their matching papers of a bullseye and with an axe wedged in the center. "We both got axe-throwing for our activity!" said Cyrano, excitedly.

"Cool," answered Dooley. "Have fun."

"Okay. We'll see you at lunch," said Cyrano.

Elenore peered over her reading glasses to look at Dooley as he approached the nearly empty fishbowls. "Your turn, Dooley," she said.

"You know," he started, trying to think of some way of beginning the conversation he actually wanted to have. "I used to have a fishbowl like this. I won a goldfish at a county fair one summer when I was six," said Dooley.

"Fish are very interesting creatures. I've recently been learning about koi."

"The big goldfish people keep in those fake ponds?"

"They're actually related to carp. You can find them all over China and Japan. Gorgeous fish, don't you think? Did you know that some koi can live to be 200 years old?"

"Really?" said Dooley. "That seems pretty old for a fish. I don't think my goldfish even made it to Christmas." Dooley still hadn't picked from the two bowls. He was trying to think of exactly what he wanted to ask Elenore.

Elenore took off her reading glasses and smiled at him. "Is there something you need, Dooley?"

"Yes, actually I wanted to ask you a question if that's okay."

"I'd be happy to help. Come and sit down." She sat on the concrete base of the flagpole and gestured for Dooley to sit next to her.

"Is there such a thing as a power that lets you change from a human into an animal?" he asked.

Elenore thought for a moment. "Shape shifting? Yes, it's possible. Years ago when I was a camper here, there was a girl named Hazel who could change herself into a squirrel… well, sort of a squirrel. She could make her skin covered in the softest fur, and she could grow a tail. It was very impressive. I should look up Hazel and see what she's doing now." Elenore made a note on the paper attached to the clipboard.

"But what about someone who could change completely into an animal?"

"That's a dangerous idea. Our gifts are powerful. We have to learn to control them so they won't control us. Giving yourself over to it might involve complications. Why do you ask?"

"You know that Golden Retriever that hangs out with Counselor Busby a lot?"

"Yes."

"It's actually a human—or it used to be a human—named Caleb."

"How do you know this?" she asked.

"Virgil told me what he was saying." Dooley watched Elenore as she stared forward, absorbing his words. "Have you ever heard of Jenny Johansson?"

She turned her head quickly to look at Dooley. "Yes. Jenny Johansson lived here when it was a logging camp. Her mother was the camp cook."

"One of her brothers started this camp and the other one is a Golden Retriever," Dooley said.

"Remarkable," she said softly. "What is your power, Dooley?"

"I'm a Visus."

"A seer of the unseen. And how long have you been at Camp Pukwudgee?"

"It's Wednesday, so this is my fourth day here."

Elenore wore an expression of surprised delight. "You've uncovered a lot in a short time." She stood up and removed her reading glasses. "Those who raise koi like to give them classifications, describe their color patterns and types of scales. If you were a koi, you'd be a *tategoi*."

"What does that mean?" asked Dooley.

"A small koi with great potential."

Twenty-Three

ACTING KOI

"Choose your assignments and then come with me," instructed Elenore. "I want to show you something."

Dooley picked sweeping the boys' cabins for his chore and animal tracking for his activity. Elenore looked at his slips—one with a picture of a broom and one with a picture of a paw print—and took out a pocket-sized book from the picnic basket sitting near them. "You'll need this when you join your group to track animal footprints in the forest." Dooley silently read the book cover, *The Bloodstone Forest: A Field Guide* by F. Boone. He slipped the book into the back pocket of his shorts. "Now," said Elenore, "let's head over to the meeting lodge before I have to start my first lesson in the dojo."

They walked into the lodge, passed the large meeting room with several rows of folding chairs facing a raised stage and into an equipment room in the back. There were croquet sets and giant beach balls and a rack full of costumes. Elenore pushed aside a cardboard box labeled WIGS and said, "Aha! Here it is!" She opened a blue plastic bin and bent over it, rummaging inside it until she stood up holding a heavy book over her head, triumphantly. "This should help answer your questions about Caleb."

Dooley looked at the book in his hands. It had a protective book cover made of brown paper. "I'm not really much of a reader," he said.

"I purchased this book at an estate sale several years ago," said Elenore, ignoring his reluctance. "I can't say that I've read it personally, but if that dog really is Caleb Johansson, it may explain why he seems to be stuck in this animal state."

"Thank you," he said, trying to hide the disappointment he felt. He was hoping for something more helpful than a long, dull book.

"My pleasure, Dooley." Elenore turned to leave, and Dooley followed her out of the equipment room and the meeting room.

Just before they descended the steps of the front porch, Dooley said, "Sensei Elenore, about those koi…"

"Yes?"

"How could they live to be 200 years old? And how did they know the fish were that old?"

"Good questions," she said. "You know how you can count the rings on a tree to see how old it is? Well, you can do the same thing with koi. They have microscopic rings on their scales that show how many summers and winters they've lived." Elenore adjusted her kimono and brushed a few stands of silver hair from her forehead. "And as for how they could live that long, no one really knows. Maybe it's because they swim in the clearest, cleanest water or maybe it's because they have caretakers who tend to their needs very carefully or maybe because they don't know any differently so they remain healthy and hopeful for the next day to be just as good as the last."

"Sounds boring to me," said Dooley.

"It's a good thing you're not a fish," she said, patting him gently on the arm.

Dooley watched her walk down the steps and past the flagpole to the craft dojo. He flipped the book open to the title page. "*Therianthropy: The Gift of Shape Shifting*," he read aloud. Sighing, he tucked the book under his arm and descended the steps. Just as Dooley was about to pass the dojo, Elenore slid open the door and called to him. "Oh, Dooley!"

"Yes," he answered.

"For the tracking activity, I forgot to say that if you have a compass, you might want to get it from your cabin. Counselor Boone—your forest guide—has a few, but since you're running a bit behind, they may all be gone. It's easy to get turned around in a dark forest."

"Oh, thank you!" Dooley exclaimed.

Dooley ran to his cabin and threw the heavy book on his sleeping bag. He pulled his backpack out from under his bunk and quickly unzipped the front pocket to find his compass. Grateful for Elenore's advice, he grasped the old brass object tightly as he ran out of the cabin and toward the forest. He wanted to complete his assignments quickly

so he could get back to the quiet of his cabin and learn all
he could about Caleb the Golden Retriever.

Twenty-Four

A FIELD GUIDE

Dooley joined the five campers assembled in a clearing just at the edge of the forest. A barrel-chested man wearing green camouflage from head to foot stood in the center of the group. He had a scraggly brown beard and bushy eyebrows which nearly hid his small, dark eyes. He spoke with a thick Southern accent. "My name is Fowler Boone. I'm the head of forestry and beekeeping at Camp Pukwudgee. You'll call me Boone if'n you have a reason to call me at all." Boone spat on the ground and continued, "Take out your field guides, and I'll show you what animals we'll be tracking today."

Dooley took the small book out of his back pocket and opened it to the Table of Contents.

"As you open to the first page," Boone continued, "you'll note that this is no ordinary field guide. This handy-dandy little book will show how to measure the size and stride of an animal's prints, along with looking for identifiers such as claw imprints. There's also an entire chapter about animal scat—that's poop to you newbies. This guide will help you identify the tracks of common forest animals versus those creatures seen mainly in our neck o' the woods.

Section One—Raccoon or Teakettler?

Section Two—Bobcat or Wampus?

Section Three—Black Bear or Gumberoo?

Section Four—Wild Turkey or Hodag?

And so forth and so on."

Boone distributed a handful of stubby yellow pencils. "At the back of the book, there are blank pages for you to record your findings. You will sketch what tracks you find and make out which animal it's from. You'll need at least six tracks to complete this activity. If you can find all of the prints in the field guide, you'll get ten extra points toward the triple P—the Perfect Pukwudgee Participant award. As you explore the Bloodstone Forest, it's important to remain as silent as a Whirling Whimpus turned to syrup, understood? Alrighty. Any questions? No? Then find you a partner and get busy tracking."

"I have a question," Dooley said softly to himself as he leafed through the pages of the field guide. "What's a Whirling Whimpus?"

"Right?" Sama was standing beside him. "I don't know how I've avoided choosing the tracking activity in all my years at camp, but here I am."

"Do you have a partner yet?" Dooley asked.

"No," Sama answered.

"How about we pair up and get this done really quickly?

I've got this," he said, showing Sama his compass. "It's actually a magic compass, bewitched to show you which way to go according to what you're looking for."

"Where did you get that?" she asked, surprised.

"It's a long story that I'll tell you about later. Right now let's just get this over with. With this compass and your power to hear what others can't, maybe this won't be too hard."

Sama agreed. They both studied the spinning letters and quivering red-tipped needle. Dooley silently asked the compass to show him what he needed to find in the forest. A moment later, the letters stopped and the needle pointed to the N.

"So how do you know which way to go now?" asked Sama.

"We always go southeast, or actually S.E."

"And you know this because…"

"Like I said—long story. It involves a Valkyrie and a Viking warlord she called a *skapraun eptri*, which means 'annoying backside.'" Dooley didn't feel like explaining. "Just trust me."

"Okay."

As they hiked deeper into the forest, they concentrated only on the compass, never noticing that the other camper partners stayed closer to the clearing at the edge of the forest.

Twenty-Five

ALWAYS GO S.E.

"**A**re you sure this thing knows where we should go?" asked Sama after they had been walking for twenty minutes. "We haven't seen any tracks yet."

"Maybe it's taking us to some really rare footprints," Dooley answered, hopefully.

They continued to move deeper into the forest, staring at the ground while occasionally glancing at the compass to be sure they were continuing in the right direction.

Sama looked up at the heavy tree canopy above them. "It's so dark. It's hard to see anything."

They approached a broad, decaying log lying next to a splintered stump. The log was slick with green moss and covered in rows of shelf-like yellow fungi. Dooley climbed over it, followed by Sama. On the other side of the log, they were surprised to find that the ground sloped down into a steep crater. They skidded clumsily until they reached the bottom of the hole with a thump.

"What is this?" exclaimed Dooley, as he stood and brushed off the seat of his shorts. "This hole must be like eight-feet deep. It looks like it was hit by a meteor."

The crater was surrounded by tall walls of packed dirt and exposed tree roots. They examined the circle of blackened soil beneath their feet. At its center there was an even deeper hole. Dooley dug around it with the toe of his sneaker.

"Do you think we can climb out?" asked Sama.

"I think so. If we grab on to these roots, we can pull ourselves out."

Sama searched for a loose root to use as a rope. She found one and tugged it forcefully, checking that it was anchored securely.

"What did you say, Dooley?" asked Sama, the root still in her hands.

"I didn't say anything," Dooley responded. He was crouched down by the smaller hole now, sifting through the black dirt and making the hole deeper.

Sama grabbed Dooley's arm, pulling him up to his feet. "Dooley," Sama said softly, "It's Jenny. She's here."

Dooley spun around to look for Jenny. "Where? I don't see her."

"She says to look up—on the log."

Dooley took a step back to see the log they had climbed over before sliding into the crater. He saw Jenny sitting with her legs and bare feet dangling over the side. She waved and smiled sadly at Dooley. Dooley waved back.

"What is this place?" he asked.

"She says it's a dark place," Sama answered. "The place where it all began."

"What do you mean? Where what all began?"

"We used to be close—the three of us," repeated Sama. "We were the only children at the lumber camp, so we were each other's only friends." Dooley watched Jenny's movements—her lips and her eyes and her hands—as she spoke. He adjusted to the delay from Jenny's mouth to Sama's recitation.

"You and your brothers?"

"Yes. Of course, I was the oldest and the only girl, so I was expected to help Momma in the big kitchen. There wasn't as much playtime for me. But I knew we were different. I knew we had powers. I tried to teach the boys how to use their gifts, to control them, but they wouldn't always listen to me. That is, until the time they should've just ignored my instructions."

"What happened in this spot?" Dooley asked. He felt that familiar shiver run down his neck, shoulders and arms. "Why is this a dark place? Is it because... because this is where you died?"

Jenny stopped swinging her legs and folded her arms across her chest. "Heavens, no. This is the spot where I began to live forever."

Twenty-Six

EVERETT JOHANSSON

Dooley gave Jenny a questioning look, wondering what she meant.

"You have learned some of our story," Sama continued repeating Jenny's words, "but there is still much you don't know."

"Please, tell me," Dooley pleaded. "I want to help you."

Jenny unfolded her arms and smoothed her pinafore apron. She pointed to the *J* stitched on the pocket. "My mother stitched this *J*, just as she sewed all of my clothes." Sama sat on the ground cross-legged and closed her eyes to concentrate on Jenny's story. "Both my parents were hard workers. Momma used to tell me how my father, Everett Johansson, had been a lumberjack since he was a boy. Over the years, he had different jobs in the lumber camp. Pa was a whistle punk who watched for the safety of the other men and blew his whistle when a log got loose or the arm of the yarder swung fitfully or the steam logging machine looked to blow. When he first started, he was a high climber who could scramble up the spar tree as easily as a red squirrel. Later, when Pa was foreman, it was his job to pick the spar tree—the tallest and strongest tree to climb and top off. Selecting that spar tree was so important seeing that all the other trees were attached to it with cables."

Dooley sat down on the ground, leaning against the dirt wall so he could look at Jenny while she spoke. "Did your parents have powers, too?" he asked her.

"It's hard to say," Jenny answered through Sama. "At least, they never told me as much, but people found Momma to be a little odd—she wouldn't talk much in front of strangers—and my father died when I was still young. Most of what I know of him is from the stories Momma told us. Now that I've had so many years to think on this, there are times I wonder if Pa did have a power. Momma and the other men at the camp told tales of him felling trees just by sneezing on them. They'd say he could lasso tree limbs and tie them up like a spider's web to make himself a hammock and take a nap. But maybe that's all they were, just tales—tall tales—told to a trusting, little girl by weary loggers."

"What happened to your father?" Dooley asked.

"There were many ways for a lumberjack to die in a lumber camp, but there were two things we knew all too well: men got sick and men got hurt. There was a man in camp named Whispering Dan. Some of the men who came to work as lumberjacks changed their names. Many had sad and regretful pasts they were leaving behind, so they gave themselves new names. I don't know what Dan's name was before, but he was given the 'whispering' part as a joke for he was the loudest man around. He was loud when he ate. He was loud when he worked. He was loud when he slept. And in between, he was just plain loud—bellowing at everybody. You ever met a person who acts like he knows everything but actually knows little to nothing?"

Dooley nodded.

"Well, that was Whispering Dan. And a lumberjack like that is a danger just as powerful as a lightning storm. It was early spring—the time when the men floated the logs down the river to the sawmill. The snow had melted, and the Hache River was high. All winter long, the men had been piling up the logs far upstream, and Dan's job was to make sure there was a clear path for them to roll down and into the river. Momma said that Dan was lazy and didn't believe what Pa told him to do was important. He thought he knew better than everybody else, even my father. When it was time to release the logs, they got hung on the rocks and bushes in their path. Once my father saw what had happened, he ordered one of his men to go fetch Pint-Size Pat. He was small and quick as a jackrabbit. Pa wanted Pat to find the key log, the one hung on something that was causing the jam, and take it out. Reckless, Dan didn't wait for Pint-Size Pat. He climbed up there first and caused the whole thing to come tumbling down with Pa still in the way. Whispering Dan lost his left arm that day, but my father lost his life."

Twenty-Seven

VISION BUSH

"Your poor mother," said Sama to Jenny. "She must've been heartbroken."

"Yeah," Dooley agreed. "Was she able to stay at the camp as the cook?"

"They felt sorry for my mother, raising three kids alone." Sama continued to recite Jenny's story. "Peter was a baby when Pa died in 1901. Caleb was three, and I was just seven years old. The company that owned the sawmill let her stay on as cook until they closed down the lumber camp nearly ten years later."

"So, if you didn't die, but you were born in," Dooley did the math in his head, "1894, how are you still here? I mean… are you alive or something else?" asked Dooley.

"I suppose it's something else," answered Jenny through Sama.

Dooley waited to see if Jenny would offer more information. When she didn't, he asked, "Does it have to do with your power? Do you have a special ability to live forever?"

"It has more to do with my brother Peter. Peter was the youngest and a bit spoiled by Momma, I think. She saw early on that he could grow things—peculiar plants and flowers foreign to this place. Banana trees growing during dark winter months. And he had a second power, too. He could see things hidden to the eyes of others. He grew a bush—he called it his Vision Bush. It had yellow berries with blue and green spots that he would crush into a paste. He used the paste to make a special ink that could only be seen by people with this power."

"So Peter was what we call a Greenie—someone who can do magical things with plants and a Visus—someone who can see things not seen by others," said Dooley. "And I know about your brother Caleb and his power to turn himself into a dog. What about you? What's your power?"

"I'm also a—what was the word—a Visus, though my ability has faded over the years. I used to be able to see the creatures of these woods before they were nearby. I could see the future. When Momma took note of what I could do, she discouraged it. She was afraid of what the others would think about her strange children."

"You can't blame her for being nervous after all she'd been through," said Dooley.

"Yes. I suppose so. But I found that I had other powers, too. I could make myself hidden so that no one could find me. It would seem as though I had vanished."

"A Skrito," answered Dooley, impressed.

"And if I concentrated real hard and a person was willing,

I could speak to them with my mind. I could send my brothers pictures and scenes."

"Doo-ley! Sa-ma!" A voice called to them from somewhere in the forest.

"It sounds like Counselor Boone," Sama replied. "I totally forgot about the tracking activity."

"We're in a hole!" Dooley shouted. "Down here!"

Jenny stood up from the log where she had been sitting. She turned her head side-to-side, searching around her with wide open eyes.

"Wait!" Dooley said. "Don't leave. It's just one of our counselors. He won't hurt you."

"She says she has to go," said Sama.

"I still have so many questions. When can we talk again? You haven't told us why this is a dark place!" Frustrated, Dooley watched Jenny leave the edge of the hole. "Did she say anything else?" Dooley asked Sama.

"She said she'd explain another time."

A rope with fat knots at even intervals dropped down into the hole. "Grab on, campers," came Boone's gruff voice from above. "I'll get you outta there in two clicks of a Snallygaster's bill."

Boone hauled Sama out, followed by Dooley. Standing on the fallen log, Dooley looked around for any sign of Jenny, but she had disappeared.

THURSDAY

Twenty-Eight

CANTATA LIBER

Something small and green hit Dooley on the nose and woke him up. Looking at the object which had been thrown at him, now resting on his chest, he saw it was the string doll Cyrano had made for him at the craft dojo.

"Dooley," Leo called from the top bunk. "Shut up! You're talking in your sleep. You're gonna wake up the whole cabin."

"What time is it?" asked Dooley, judging by the light barely spilling into the room that it was just after dawn.

"I don't know but it's too early!" Leo growled.

The mattress springs above Dooley groaned as Leo rolled over, attempting to go back to sleep. Dooley's head felt groggy and his muscles were sore. Seeing his sleeping bag pushed to the foot of his bed and his pillow on the dusty concrete floor beneath him made Dooley realize he had slept uneasily.

As the fog lifted from his mind, he remembered a dream: he was alone and at the bottom of the hole, only it was much wider and deeper than the one they had found in the Bloodstone Forest. He was shouting for help, but no one came at first. Then a face appeared. It was Tristen. Dooley asked her for a rope or a branch to pull him out of the hole, but Tristen pelted him with pinecones instead. More faces were added to the rim of the hole—Cyrano, Leo, Sama, Celeste—and they threw pinecones, too. Finally, Jenny was there. She spoke in a different voice, not Sama's, and said, "If it were not for hope, the heart would break. Build hopefulness, adding a little more to what you had the day before." The pinecones multiplied beneath his feet until Dooley was able to step out of the now-filled hole.

Dooley sighed, trying to shift his thoughts to the reality of being awake and away from his dream. He pulled his sleeping bag toward him, situating himself inside it, and reached for his pillow. Under his pillow, Dooley found the book Elenore had lent him. He picked it up, raised himself to a seated position and placed the heavy book in his lap. The book cover was blank and felt like it was made of brown paper grocery bags. He ran his finger along the worn spine of the book, noting tears and marks. He opened to the title page and read to himself: *Wake Up, Sleepyhead! Dream Interpretation for Dummies.*

Surprised, Dooley closed the book quickly. He was sure the book Elenore gave him was about people turning themselves into animals. He paused, then reached under his bed for his backpack and took out his flashlight. He switched it on, shining light on the closed book. Dooley slowly opened the book again. This time, the title page read, *Cantata Liber:*

How to Use a Visus Encyclopedia. Dooley turned to the next page and read the introduction:

Greetings, Fortunate Reader! You have in your hands a reference book only accessible to those gifted with the power of Unseen Sight. To anyone not in possession of the Visus Eye, this enchanted book will fill its pages with impossibly complex and frustratingly circuitous mathematical equations which will automatically cause the non-Visus reader to immediately set the book down and take a nap. To use this book, concentrate on a question and open the book to find information about that subject. For example, before you opened the book just now, you were asking yourself, "What is this book?" The following pages offer an in-depth explanation to answer this question.

Good luck, fellow Visus! Keep asking questions!
Sincerely,
Prof. Charles T. Oculus

Twenty-Nine

MY WEEK AS A SALAMANDER

Dooley continued reading until the other Jackalope campers began to wake up.

"Is that the book Sensei Elenore gave you?" asked Cyrano as he sniffed a t-shirt he had pulled out of his duffel bag, testing its odor to determine if it could be worn two days in a row.

"Yep," Dooley answered. "It's pretty amazing." Dooley explained how the book filled its pages with information according to what questions the reader might have.

"So now you know all about Shape Shifters?"

"I definitely know more than I did before, which was nothing. According to this book, Caleb must've been a really talented one. It's unusual for them to be able to completely change into an animal without keeping some human characteristics. In each chapter, the author of this book interviews people with the gift of Therianthropy—you know, changing into animals—to get their perspective."

Cyrano sat down on the bed next to Dooley. "Does the book talk about why someone might be stuck as an animal? That's what we're thinking happened to Caleb, right?"

"There's a chapter about that." Dooley flipped through the pages. "Here it is: *Chapter 14, My Week as a Salamander.* This guy—Bobby Jenkins was his name—worked for years to turn himself into a salamander. He kept a diary about it. There's a story about this one time when he was mostly a salamander—he still had a human head—and his cat, Muffin, caught him. He started barking at her so she'd put him down. Crazy. Eventually, he got all the way there, completely salamanderized."

"Is that even a word?" Cyrano asked.

"I dunno, but anyway, Bobby was like that for a week."

"How did he get back to normal?"

"There was a spell. Bobby's mother was a Rhymer, and she brought him back with a spell." Dooley shut the book and smiled at Cyrano. "I think we need to talk to Clio about this. She's a Rhymer, so maybe she can figure out how to make Caleb a human again." Dooley slid the book under his pillow.

"It's worth a try, I guess." Cyrano stood up and looked at Leo, still asleep. "Should we wake him up?"

"Nah. Let's leave him. He didn't sleep very well, and it's kinda my fault. I'll bring him back some toast or something."

Dooley and Cyrano got dressed quickly. As soon as the boys had walked down the steps of the front porch of the

Jackalope cabin, they were greeted by Tristen.

"Good morning, Sack-o-Dopes!" she jeered.

"That's *Jackalopes*, Tristen," Cyrano responded humorlessly. "Get it right."

"Whatever," said Tristen. "Dooley, I heard what happened to you in the Bloodstone Forest. Sama told me everything. What are you going to do now?"

"I'm going to eat breakfast," said Dooley, grinning.

Tristen stepped in front of Dooley and turned to stand toe-to-toe with him. "Don't mess with me, little boy." Tristen poked her pointer finger into Dooley's chest. "When I solve this mystery about the Ghost Girl and her shape-shifting younger brother, I will get the Triple P award for an unprecedented ninth year in a row. And in the meantime, I will expand my knowledge of powers, taking me one step closer to adding a third power to my already formidable arsenal of magical abilities." She stepped back from Dooley and brushed off something invisible from his shoulder. "I'll let you help me, but don't get in my way."

The boys watched Tristen walk towards the Mess Hall.

"That's really nice of Tristen to let you help her, seeing as how she wouldn't know any of this without you," Cyrano said, sarcastically.

"Hey, what's that?" Dooley spied a dark stone among a jumble of other rocks on the edge of the path. He picked it up, admiring its colors and luster. About the size of a large walnut, it was streaked with red and blackish-green. It felt cold in his hand and as smooth as a marble.

"Dooley! You got the bloodstone!" cried Cyrano.

Dooley slipped the stone in his pocket, wondering what other surprises his fifth day at Camp Pukwudgee would bring.

Thirty

FOREVER

Dooley spotted Clio while standing in the breakfast line. She was sitting with Sama and the rest of the girls from the Wendigo cabin. They all leaned forward, listening to Sama talk. Dooley couldn't hear what she was saying, but he assumed it was an account of their experience in the forest with Jenny from the day before.

"I wish Sama wouldn't broadcast Jenny's story to everybody," said Dooley.

"Why not?" asked Cyrano, hungrily eyeing the food the cooks were serving to the campers ahead of them in line.

"I don't know. It just feels like we need to keep this quiet for a bit."

He was watching the group so intently that he didn't notice that Counselor Busby was standing beside him until he tapped Dooley on the shoulder.

"Dooley?" Busby said.

"Oh!" Dooley jumped slightly.

"Counselor Busby, you're back!"

"Yes. I had to make a quick visit to see a relative."

"Bagel or muffin?" Blanche, one of the kitchen cooks, asked Dooley.

"Bagel, please." She handed Dooley his food.

"Can I get you anything, Counselor Busby?" Blanche asked. Her face reddened all the way from her chin to her hair net.

"No, thank you. I already ate."

"Suit yourself," she responded, disappointed.

"Dooley, would you mind stepping outside for a moment? Perhaps you could eat your bagel on the steps of the mess hall."

"I'll grab something for Leo," Cyrano said.

"This way, Dooley," Busby directed. Dooley complied, though he was anxious to speak to Clio. There were wicker rocking chairs dispersed along the mess hall's porch which wrapped around both sides and the front of the building. Dooley followed Busby to one of the sides and sat down next to him.

"Virgil Lee told me about your conversation with Caleb. You can imagine my surprise when I found out that I had been living so closely to my great-great uncle for all these years. It was quite a shock. I wanted to see what else I could find out about my Great-grandfather Peter and his siblings, so I went to speak to my Aunt Claudine who lives in a nursing home in St. Cloud."

"Was she able to give you any new information?" asked Dooley.

"I hadn't visited her in some time, so I didn't realize how disorientated she's become. She's very old, nearly 100 years old. She was my grandmother's sister."

"So, Peter was her father?"

"That's right."

"Did she ever live at the camp?"

"No. Claudine was born after they moved away from here."

Dooley's shoulders drooped and his plate nearly slid off his lap.

"It's curious how the mind works, Dooley. The only thing she said that I could understand was a quote from a poem. She said, 'Forever is composed of nows.' I suppose it was an answer to my questions about the past."

Dooley tore a chunk off his dry bagel. "I guess so," he said.

"If I'm not mistaken, that's from a poem by Emily Dickinson."

Dooley looked up. "Sir?"

"'Forever is composed of nows' is from the poet Emily Dickinson. I'm impressed that dear, old Claudine can still remember it." Busby stood up from the rocker. "Oh, I nearly forgot to mention… I heard you got the stone."

"The stone?" Dooley had already forgotten the smooth stone in his pocket.

"Yes. I heard you found the bloodstone. It's one of my favorite Camp Pukwudgee traditions. The Waddle-dee-wop may sound like nonsense, but it's an old rhyme passed down through my family."

"I didn't know that, Counselor Busby."

Busby squared his shoulders proudly. "Speaking of the

bloodstone, when you go into the forest to put the stone in the tamarack tree, be very careful. Counselor Boone told me this morning that two campers fell into a very deep hole yesterday. I suspect there's a female Gumberoo getting her nest ready for a new litter of cubs. They like to keep their babies in deep holes for some reason. Well, good luck!"

Thirty-One

CREATIVITY TAKES COURAGE

Dooley joined Cyrano and Leo at the flagpole waiting to choose their activities from the fishbowls. Leo was wadding up the paper muffin liner from the blueberry muffin he'd just finished eating.

"Hey, Leo," said Dooley. "Sorry about being so loud this morning."

"No worries. Leonardo Rembrandt Johnson doesn't hold a grudge." Leo tossed the paper in a nearby trashcan. "I heard you got the bloodstone. When are you going to say the Waddle-dee-wop?"

Dooley put his hand in his shorts pocket. He grasped the stone and rubbed it with his thumb. "Oh, I don't know."

"You're not scared, are you?" Cyrano asked. "I mean, it's not like you've never been in the Bloodstone Forest before."

Cyrano leaned in to whisper to Dooley. "And you can bring the compass to find the tamarack tree faster."

"Yeah," Dooley agreed. "That's a good idea."

After Busby's morning announcements, each camper chose a slip from the fishbowls.

"I got the craft dojo and the nurse's clinic," Dooley told Leo and Cyrano.

"Lucky!" Cyrano cried. "You get to sort the nurse's band-aids by cartoon character! There's like a thousand of them and they come in a big box, but she likes them to be more organized."

"Sounds fun," Dooley said, feigning excitement.

"Well, it's better than setting skunk traps with Counselor Boone which is what I got for a chore," Cyrano said.

"I got crafts, too," said Leo. "I'll walk over there with you."

Leo and Dooley said goodbye to Cyrano and stopped by the cabin before heading to the craft dojo. Dooley felt a calming balance with the bloodstone in one pocket and the compass in the other.

"Ohayou!" Elenore greeted them at the door of the dojo, cooling herself with a brightly colored fan. She wore slim-cut blue pants and a tunic-length royal blue shirt with two tropical birds embroidered across on the front and red piping along the collar.

"That means 'good morning' in Japanese," Leo told Dooley.

"Ohayou," the boys repeated.

"Sensei Elenore, is it okay if I take Dooley back to the painting studio and show him what I'm working on?" Leo asked.

"Of course!" she responded cheerfully.

Leo led Dooley past the kitchen and into the studio full of canvases sitting on easels. At the side of the room, there was a card table covered with a splatter-painted drop cloth. Leo lifted the cloth and said, "Voila!"

Before him, Dooley saw a bust made of various recycled items. The head was a red, rubber kickball. The eyes were metal washers with a blue button glued inside one washer and a blue marble glued inside the other. Two rows of white Tic-Tac candies were glued near the bottom like teeth. The hair was thick braids made of rope, string and purple yarn. Glittery silver and purple pipe cleaners were formed into a tiara that sat lightly on top of the coils of hair.

"I'm stumped on what to use for her nose," said Leo. "What do you think?"

"Umm…"

"Because, you know Beryl has the cutest nose…"

"So, it's Beryl?"

Leo looked insulted. "Isn't it obvious?"

"Yes. Sure. I can see it now," Dooley answered. "But why do you keep trying to make art for Beryl? Aren't afraid of what might happen when she or her friends see it?"

"The great French artist Henri Matisse once said, 'Creativity takes courage,'" Leo responded. "I invited Beryl to come over this morning to see my creation, so I need all the courage I can get. How about, instead of making me more nervous, you help me find something for her nose?"

"Deal."

Thirty-Two

A LITTLE UNDERSTANDING

By the time Dooley and Leo had plucked a leaf from the rhododendron bush outside the craft dojo and glued it in the middle of the kickball meant to be Beryl's face, Leo was jumpy and anxious.

"What do you think?" he asked Dooley. "Do you think she'll like it?"

"Yeah. Probably. I mean, what girl wouldn't want a recycled art sculpture of her head, right?"

The boys heard a girl's voice in the kitchen. Leo threw the drop cloth back over his artwork and sat down on a stool trying to act as casual and unconcerned as possible. Dooley could see he was ready to bolt out of the room.

As Clio and Beryl entered the painting studio, Clio was signing something to Beryl then Beryl signed a response back.

"We are here, geek," said Clio, "and we don't have all week."

Leo cleared his throat and stood up. "I give you…" He lifted the cloth with a flourish. "Princess Beryl of Puckwudgee!"

Dooley watched as Beryl gave Leo a half-smile which turned into a full smile, highlighting the deep dimple on her left cheek.

"Oh! I almost forgot!" Leo grabbed a pretzel and broke off a small, curved piece. He glued it on to the side of the kickball. "Your dimple," he said, pointing to the pretzel.

Beryl leaned forward and kissed him on the cheek. Clio spoke and signed at the same time, "Beryl, don't encourage the weirdo! He'll follow you wherever you go!"

Beryl looked at Dooley, then signed something to Clio. Clio signed back and said, "Beryl says she senses your fear. She says for you to come here." Beryl motioned for Dooley to sit on the stool next to where she was standing. Once he was seated, Beryl signed again, and Clio said, "Sit still and think watery blue thoughts. She'll try to speak to your mind and untie its worried knots."

Beryl sat on a stool facing Dooley so that their knees were touching. She held both of Dooley's hands and rested her head against his head. As he closed his eyes, Dooley could hear Leo exhale loudly and make a small grumbling noise which sounded like "not fair."

Watery blue, Dooley thought. He conjured in his mind a memory of standing on the edge of an ocean and staring at an endless expanse of blue water. After a few minutes, he felt like he was plunging into the water, but instead of feeling wet and cold, Dooley felt only warmth. As he sunk deeper into the blue, the colors intensified and darkened.

"Hello, Dooley," came a voice somewhere just behind or above him, he couldn't be sure where it was coming from. "It's me, Beryl."

As soon as she said her name, everything around Dooley changed. The still blue water exploded. Now Dooley was resting on an ocean floor in the midst of a kingdom of coral formations in every color imaginable.

"Don't be afraid. I'm a Telephone, so I'm just going to use my power talk to you." With each word, a tiny, vibrant fish swam past his face. "I have felt the vibration of Jenny's presence for some time—a checkered pattern of greens and pinks and waves of soft reddish-browns—but I didn't know what or who she was. With the new information we have, I want you to remember a few things so you can understand her better."

The fish chased each other until they were gone. Then Dooley saw a giant turtle swimming toward him and Beryl continued, "Jenny is lonely. She misses what it feels to be fully alive. She wants things to change. She wants to feel something besides cold and sad. She feels great guilt." The turtle swam away, its flippers paddling against the current slowly and deliberately. "She wants to move on." Watching the turtle grow smaller as it swam away, Dooley saw a famil- iar design on its shell. The color and the mottled pattern reminded him of the bloodstone. "Find the spell, Dooley."

The moment Dooley heard his name, he was trans- ported back to the painting studio with a yank. He gasped, sputtering as if he was coming out of an unexpected wave.

"Clio, I need to ask you—is it possible that the Waddle-dee-wop is a spell?"

Thirty-Three

WADDLE-DEE-WOP

Dooley pulled a piece of sketch paper from a recycling bin and a pencil from a coffee can. "So how does it go?"

"How does what go?" asked Leo.

"The Waddle-dee-wop. What are the words?"

"Waddle-dee-wop, ploddle-dee-plum…" Leo began.

"No, not the made-up words," said Dooley. "Tell me the ending of each line."

Clio cleared her throat with an air of authority and recited, "Count to one and cut your thumb. Count to two and stir the brew. Count to three and skin your knee. Count to four and shout for more. Count to five and come alive."

"That could be a spell, couldn't it?" Dooley asked. "It ends with 'come alive.' Maybe it's supposed to bring Jenny back to life."

Clio sighed heavily. "Just because there's a rhyme doesn't make it a spell every time."

Dooley studied the phrases he had written. "Counselor

Busby said the Waddle-dee-wop was handed down for generations in his family—Jenny's family. Maybe this is a spell, but some of the words have changed over the years."

"Yeah! Like how the words to nursery rhymes can change over time," added Leo. "I used to think that in 'Row, Row, Row Your Boat' it said, 'Life's a butter dream.'" Leo looked at the faces of his friends for confirmation of what he assumed was a common misconception but saw only puzzled expressions.

"Anyway…" Dooley stood up. "Leo, will you write down the beginning parts for each line? I'm going to go put the bloodstone in the tamarack tree and see what happens."

Dooley slid open the door to the craft dojo, walked to the edge of the forest and stared into its darkening shadows. He held up his bewitched compass and said, "Show me the tamarack tree." The letters and the needle on the compass spun in opposite directions until they stopped. When Dooley saw the red-tipped needle pointing north, he started off in the direction of S.E.

Dooley remembered Sama saying she could hear the Hache River nearby when she was looking for the tamarack tree, but the compass was leading him away from the river. He decided to trust the compass, and after walking for several minutes through the dense woods, Dooley stepped into a spot cleared of the usual sugar maple and red oak trees. The mid-morning sun beamed down into the sparse space and onto a tall tree with light green needles and tiny, reddish pinecones. "This must be it," said Dooley. "But where are the holly bushes? Sama said there would be holly bushes around it."

Dooley returned his compass to his back pocket and took out the bloodstone and the paper with the words to the Waddle-dee-wop. He backed up and sat down on a moss-covered boulder to decide what to do next, looking up at the tree.

Suddenly a high-pitched whistle sounded, followed by the sound of an animal tearing through the forest. His heart beating wildly, Dooley slid off his seat on the boulder and hid behind it. In a moment he saw Caleb, the Golden Retriever, crashing through a thicket of viburnum bushes. Caleb stopped by the side of the tamarack tree and began digging a hole which Dooley assumed he'd use to hide in. Just as he was about to call Caleb to come and sit by him, Dooley saw Jenny approach.

She was running, a look of frantic concern fixed on her face. She advanced toward Caleb and knelt beside him. She reached out her hand to comfort him and ease the dog's panic but drew her hand back slowly. Caleb continued to dig, unaware of his sister's presence, throwing dirt in every direction. Dooley stepped around from his hiding place and approached the dog. "It's okay, boy," said Dooley as he patted the dog's back. "Calm down, Caleb." The dog turned quickly and bared his teeth at Dooley, growling menacingly. But once Caleb recognized Dooley, his demeanor changed and his tail began to wag.

Jenny smiled at Dooley gratefully.

"What's got you so upset, buddy?" asked Dooley as he rubbed behind Caleb's ears and on top of his head. Caleb licked Dooley's cheek in response.

"It's that teakettler call." Dooley turned to see Counselor Boone. He carried a mammoth duffel bag in camouflage green over his shoulder. He dropped the bag on the ground with a thud. "That hound gets mighty wound up when he hears it."

"I don't blame him," Dooley admitted as he adjusted the purple bandana tied around Caleb's neck which had become askew in his frightened galloping through the forest. "It's pretty creepy."

"It's not half as bad as what it's warning us about."

"I didn't know the teakettler's whistle was supposed to warn us."

"I'm not much surprised you didn't know about that considering how poorly you did at your tracking activity yesterday."

"I did fall in a hole, Counselor Boone."

"True enough." Boone opened up his bag and pulled out a coil of rope and a tightly-knit pile of netting. "The teakettler whistles when it sees a predator. I'd say that dog you got there's been attacked many times from the way it's cowering. Caleb knows to hide when he hears that whistle."

Dooley looked at Jenny. She nodded her head sadly.

"What's that?" Dooley asked, pointing to the netting and rope.

"This here's a trap. I made this to catch a gumberoo. You

got to keep the stitches real close together for a job like this, 'cause a gumberoo will slide right through if the holes are too big. Yep, them hairless bears are half-jellified bones and half teeth. And if you wake one up while he's hibernating—"

Dooley picked up the apparatus for the trap. "So you made this netting?"

"Yep."

"So, you're a Knitter?"

Boone looked at Dooley soberly. "That's my power, son. D'you think that's funny?"

"No, sir," answered Dooley. He tried not to smile as he thought about Cyrano's grandmother whose power was also knitting. He tried to imagine the two of them—gruff, camo-covered Fowler Boone and tiny, gray-haired Granny Gibbs—rocking side by side and knitting together.

Boone huffed, irritably. "You're here to put the bloodstone in the tamarack tree, aren't you? Why don't you get on with it, so the tree can move to its tomorrow-spot and we can both get on with our day?"

"The tree moves?"

Boone stuffed the netting and rope back in his duffel bag and shouldered it. "I get plum tired of you new campers. Yes, it moves as soon as you put the bloodstone in the knothole of the tree and you say the rhyme." Boone looked up at the clouds. "And I'd say from the looks of those clouds, you got a few hours before we're in the middle of a gully-washer of a thunderstorm."

Thirty-Four

HOLLOW

Once Boone was gone, Dooley walked around the tamarack tree, looking for the knothole, with Caleb jogging alongside him, panting contentedly. Jenny sat on the boulder, watching both of them. "Are you going to help me?" Dooley asked her.

Jenny smiled and shook her head.

"Fine. I'll just have to find it myself." As Dooley ran his hand over the rough tree bark, a few scale-like pieces fell away. "I'm surprised that Counselor Boone is a Knitter," said Dooley, just making conversation. "That seems like more of a power for an old lady." Jenny crossed her arms and frowned. "Oh, sorry. I guess you are an old lady…sort of, but you're not a Knitter, are you?" Dooley stopped walking around the tree and looked at Jenny. "I was just thinking; at least at some point, you had three powers—Visus, Skrito, and Telephone." Jenny crinkled her brow in a confused expression. "A Telephone is someone who can talk to others by putting images in their minds if they concentrate really hard." Jenny nodded. "Wait! Could you do that now? Could you show me what happened to you?"

Jenny stood up and bit her bottom lip. She looked around at the nearby trees, then motioned for Dooley to follow her. Dooley put the bloodstone and the piece of paper back in his pocket. They walked until they came to a shelter made from a long slab of rock balancing on two shorter rocks. Dooley had to duck to enter the little room. Observing Jenny sitting cross-legged on the carpet of leaves and pine needles, Dooley joined her, facing her as a mirror-image. Caleb sat down beside him and laid his head on his front paws.

Jenny pointed to her temple and mouthed the word *hollow*. Then, she gestured for Dooley to spread his hands in front of him and close his eyes. Dooley obeyed, trying to think of something empty and hollow. His mind quickly provided the image of the hole he and Sama had found in the Bloodstone Forest. He suddenly felt like someone had grabbed him around the waist and jerked him there. He was standing in the hole again, but this time it was deeper and the sky above him was darker and full of stars. In this dream state, Jenny appeared to Dooley. She was standing beside him in the hole. She spoke in an echoed voice, "Not here. Not yet." She grabbed his hand and he was pulled into a new place.

This time he was in an empty room. The floor, ceiling and walls were all bright white. Jenny's unchained voice said, "I don't know how long I can last, so I'll allow you three questions. Ask them quick." Dooley spun around to see Jenny standing behind him.

He was nearly overwhelmed by a dizzying sensation, like he'd just stepped off a giant rollercoaster. But he gathered his thoughts enough to say, "Okay…" and counted off his three questions. "Why are you stuck this way? Why does Caleb think this is all your fault? What did Peter lie about?"

Jenny's thumb and pointer finger came together to make a circle and she placed them against her lips to whistle loudly. A wooden bench like an old church pew appeared behind them, roughly sliding into the backs of their legs and forcing Jenny and Dooley to plop down gracelessly. In front of them, a small puppet theater appeared, complete with red velvet curtains and miniature stage lights. Two marionettes dropped onto the stage, boys with overalls—one smaller and one bigger with a purple bandana tied around his neck. Then a red-headed girl marionette joined the brothers. She wore an apron with a tiny J on the pocket. A small-scale easel holding a stack of square posters sat at one corner of the stage. The first poster read:

THE CURSE—A PLAY IN THREE ACTS

The poster fell away and the next one read:
ACT ONE—A SEED IS PLANTED

Jenny: Peter, why are you crying?
Peter: I miss our father.
Caleb: How can you miss a man you never knew?
Jenny: You were a babe in arms when Father died.
Peter: But I still feel a hollow place where his memory should be.

Jenny: Do you know what would fill up that hollow place? A scheme.

Caleb & Peter: What kind of scheme?

Jenny: A scheme to repay Whispering Dan for his blunder.

Caleb: I say we should leave that one-armed fool to himself.

Peter: Yes. Mama says we should be merciful to others.

Jenny: Let her show mercy and we will deliver justice.

The poster fell away, revealing the one behind it. It read:
ACT TWO—FULL BLOOM

Caleb's marionette was pulled up and replaced with a wolf-like creature, covered in gray fur but still wearing the overalls and purple bandana. He had a mouth full of sharp teeth and long claws.

Peter: Oh, Caleb! I do not like it when you take this form!

Beast Caleb: Beneath this disguise of a Wolf Man, a Rougarou, a Werewolf, I am still me, Little Brother. And I will not stay this way forever.

Jenny: Caleb, I will lure Dan into the forest, then it will be up to you to finish the job.

Beast Caleb: I mean only to frighten him, sister.

Peter: Yes. Mama would not like us to harm him.

Jenny's marionette stood at one end of the puppet stage and her brothers at the other, crouching behind a flat tree. A one-armed marionette descended onto center stage.

Jenny: Dan, they have sent me to fetch you. You are to go deep into the forest.

Dan: I take no orders from a little girl, but as I was

heading that way anyhow, I will go.

Jenny and Dan's marionettes walked in place as the scenery behind them rolled by and changed, the blue sky turning from azure to cobalt to a dark sapphire. Then, Beast Caleb jumped in front of them.

Beast Caleb: Roar!

Dan: A monster!

Dan's marionette fell back and hit its head on a rock. A length of red yarn, pulled by invisible fingers, was drawn from the marionette's head.

Peter: He is bleeding!

Beast Caleb: What have we done?

Jenny: We have done what is right. Whispering Dan has collected his due wages for what he did to our father seven years past.

Voices from offstage: Look! Dan is dead and he was killed by a rougarou!

The poster on the easel fell away again. The fourth poster read:

ACT THREE—WITHERING ON THE VINE

Dan is gone. Beast Caleb is replaced with Boy Caleb, and the three sibling marionettes huddled together center stage.

Peter: What should we do?

Caleb: They are coming for me!

Jenny: They do not know it was you. Quiet your fears.

Peter: Mama will know. Her heart will break when she hears what we have done.

Caleb: This is the day she has dreaded, the day her children's powers were used for evil.

Jenny: Nonsense. The men may suspect our powers, but they have no proof.

Caleb: But will we not be the first they blame?

Jenny: Perhaps. So here is what we should do: I will vanish and Caleb will take the form of a friendly dog.

Peter: And I?

Jenny: You are just a child, only eight-years old. They will not think of you. Nevertheless, you will hide in your river cave until they have finished their searching.

Caleb: But I can only fully remain in the form of a hound for a short time, a quarter of an hour at best.

Peter: And you cannot stay hidden much longer, Sister.

Jenny: Peter, you must give us some of your bewitched seeds to protect us from harm.

Peter: But they are powerful, and I know not what they will do.

Voices off stage: This way! I hear someone!

Jenny: Peter, you must give them to us now!

Peter: I will do it but take heed of this: do not lose yourself. I promise to reverse the seeds' charm if it be harmful.

A squat green bush appeared to grow in the center of the stage. Caleb and Jenny reached toward the plant. Then Caleb's marionette was replaced with one of a Golden Retriever, and Jenny's marionette disappeared.

The final poster read:

THE END.

Thirty-Five

CARRIE

Dooley felt the now familiar jerking sensation yanking him from the white room and into a new place and time—night in a quiet cabin lit by a glowing fire in a stone-arched hearth. A red-headed woman in her mid-thirties stood at a wooden table, kneading a mound of dough. She paused to wipe a strand of hair from her eyes and tuck it behind her ear, smearing flour on her cheek.

"Is that your mom?" Dooley asked.

Jenny was standing next to Dooley, also watching her mother work the lump of dough. She nodded. "Yes. That is Carrie Johansson."

"Can she hear us?"

"No. You're standing in a moment of time, one of my memories."

Dooley looked around the room. "Where are you? The *you* from this memory?"

"I'm hidden." Jenny pointed to a dark corner where

another Jenny—identical but unaware of Dooley's presence—sat on a low stool, her eyes downcast and her hands tightly clasped in her lap. "This is the night Whispering Dan was killed."

The door opened with a crash, and Peter entered the cabin. "Mama, we didn't mean to! It was an accident!"

Carrie wiped her floured hands on her apron and ran to her youngest child. "You've worried me so by coming in late! You know how it pains me to wait and wait! Tell me what's happened before I become irate!"

"We didn't mean to hurt Dan, just to scare him a little. Caleb changed into a beast and frightened Dan so that he fell and bust his head on a stone."

"Did Dan die? Son, do not lie!"

"Yes!" Peter dissolved into tears and crumpled to the floor. Carrie sat beside him and stroked his back. "The loggers came looking for him and saw Caleb's beast," Peter continued, trying to speak through choked sobs. "We were frightened and knew we should hide, so Jenny vanished and Caleb turned into a dog."

Carrie stood up and looked around the room. "Jenny, my dear, I feel you are near. Come here and appear."

Peter began sobbing harder. "She can't! I fed her seeds from the plant I've been growing, and now they're both trapped."

Carrie bent to help Peter up, leading him to a bench to sit down. She filled a metal cup with water from a hand pump and gave it to him. "This remedy may wear away. Its effects may not stay."

Peter wiped his nose on his sleeve. "This isn't like that time when Caleb changed into a dog to sit for a photograph for the man who came to the logging camp last spring. Remember, Mama? Caleb nearly changed back to himself before the man had left the room. I'm afraid this time is different. It's already been hours."

Suddenly, Dooley felt like he was spinning rapidly. He squeezed his eyes closed, and his hands clenched into fists. When the spinning stopped, he was in the same cabin, but it was daytime, and several things in the room had changed. The bare walls were now covered in pale green wallpaper. The pump on the kitchen sink had been replaced with a more modern faucet. The braided rug by the hearth was gone and a burgundy wool rug took its place. A sweet love song streamed out of a tall radio cabinet placed in the corner where Jenny had been sitting the night Carrie learned of Dan's death.

Two high-backed chairs were positioned in front of a cold fireplace. Two identical Jennys sat in the chairs, the one on the left forlornly looking at the ashes in the fireplace and the one on the right looking at Dooley. Right-side Jenny said, "Watch to understand."

Carrie sat in a jade green armchair by a window, bending slightly and humming along with the soft music. She squinted through wire-rimmed glasses at the embroidery in her lap. Her hair was still red but with streaks of gray. A sewing basket sat near her on an upholstered footstool.

A man in a navy suit with a light blue and white striped necktie opened the outside door and walked in. He took off his hat and hung it on a coat tree by the door. "Hello, Mama!" He kissed her cheek and moved the sewing basket to the floor so that he could sit on the footstool. "How's my girl?"

Carrie cupped his chin lovingly and smiled. "Peter, my dear boy, you bring me such joy."

"I've come to tell you that I got everything arranged for the camp. We're going to call it Camp Pukwudgee." Peter stood up and put his hands in his pockets, rocking back and forth on his heels. "It's going to be a place where kids can learn how to use their powers properly. And the best part is that it will keep me here," He laid his hand on her shoulder. "Closer to you."

"Peter, you fret too much over an old lady like me. It's time you took a wife and had a baby bouncing on your knee."

"There's plenty of time for that, Mama. I just needed this to be settled first."

"'In this short life that only lasts an hour,'" Carrie quoted. "'How much—how little—is within our power?'"

"There you go, quoting Emily Dickinson at me again!" Peter sat back down on the footstool. "Would you like for me to say your favorite Dickinson poem?" Peter cleared his throat and began:

Hope is the thing with feathers
That perches in the soul,
And sings the tune without the words,
And never stops at all,
And sweetest in the gale is heard;
And sore must be the storm

That could abash the little bird
That kept so many warm.
I've heard it in the chillest land,
And on the strangest sea;
Yet, never, in extremity,
It asked a crumb of me.

Carrie set down her embroidery in her lap and applauded. "I have a poem of my own to recite," she said as she took out a small stack of recipe cards bound with a blue satin ribbon from her sewing basket. "It's more of a spell, if I've done my job right." Carrie flipped each card over to look at the back until she found the right one.

Peter sighed. "Mama…"

Waddle-dee-wop, ploddle-dee-plum!
> *Count to one and cut your thumb!*
Waddle-dee-wop, faddle-dee-foo!
> *Count to two and stir the brew!*
Waddle-dee-wop, beedle-dee-bee!
> *Count to three and steep your tea!*
Waddle-dee-wop, noodle-dee-nor!
> *Count to four and feed the shag boar!*
Waddle-dee-wop, chiddle-dee-chive!
> *Count to five and learn to shrive!*

"Mama," Peter took the card from his mother and returned it to the sewing basket. "I know what this is about, but it's time we move on. This camp can be a great experience for both of us. I've spent the last three decades trying to bring them back. I've left them messages about remaining hopeful. I've traveled to foreign lands to ask advice from others." Peter laid his strong hand on his mother's aged one. "I've done all that I can for them, even though it cost me dearly. I know you still wish for a reunion, but it just isn't within my power."

They both sat without speaking, only holding hands and listening to the opening notes of the song beginning to play on the radio.

"Oh, I like this one. It's a new song by that fella Bing Crosby," said Peter. He stepped to the radio and turned up the volume to hear a crooning voice sing:

Do I want to be with you, as the years come and go?
Only forever, if you care to know.
Would I grant all your wishes and be proud of the task?
Only forever, if someone should ask...

Thirty-Six

LIGHTNING BOLT

Without warning a trapdoor opened below Dooley, and he found himself falling. Kicking his legs and flailing his arms, Dooley tried to think of what to do. He saw roots and rocks crammed into walls of packed dirt all around him. He even thought he saw the bones of some giant lizard embedded in the dirt as he continued to fall deeper into a dark abyss.

After what seemed like an hour, Dooley finally fell with a bump on solid ground. He rose to his feet, rubbing his sore backside, and looked up at a black, moonless sky. In the center of the pit, grew a scrubby, knee-high bush with blue-green pods dangling off the end of each branch.

Dooley could hear the hoots and grunts of nocturnal animals high above him and a rumbling in the clouds higher still. "Jenny?" he called.

"Here I am." Jenny floated down and stood in front of him. Her form was different, more of a silvery outline than a solid person. "My power is fading, so we must finish this quickly."

"Are we in the Bloodstone Forest?" Dooley leaned against the wall of the hole.

"Yes, but only as if in a dream."

"Is this the hole I fell in?"

"No more questions! Just listen." Jenny's voice wavered, changing from strong rebuke to a whisper. "Peter tried for years to find an antidote to his Eternity Seeds. For any other boy so young it would be too difficult a task, but he was special—smarter, kinder, braver than most. He grew other plants and bushes, feeding himself the fruit and seeds to test their effects until he finally lost his own powers. One day when he was 15-years old—nearly a man—he found that he could no longer see me. I had become invisible to his ordinary eyes. Soon after, I watched as he pulled out every dead plant in his prized garden. In trying to save us, Peter lost himself."

Loud thunder rumbled again, and a light rain began to fall.

"But years before Peter had lost his powers, he had already decided that we were cursed." The rain was falling faster now. For a brief moment a flash of lightning lit the black sky as if someone had taken their photograph, freezing Jenny's still image in Dooley's mind when he closed his eyes. A reverberating boom of thunder followed the lightning. "The day after Dan died, the plant that made the seeds that kept Caleb and me trapped in our other forms was destroyed. There was a terrible storm…" Seconds apart, a white-hot bolt of lightning and a deafening crack of thunder exploded through the air. Like a sizzling finger of electrical current, the bolt touched the bush and it was instantly reduced to ashes. "If Peter could've heard me, I'd have told him that when the lightning rid the earth of those Eternity Seeds, it also took away any chance for someone else to suffer as our family has suffered."

"If you're like this—invisible to most everyone—what are you afraid of? Why does the teakettler's whistle make you scared?"

"I'm not afraid."

"Yes, you are. Jenny, what are you afraid of?"

"I worry about him. I should've kept him safe before—"

"Who?" Dooley was shouting to be heard over the storm.

"Caleb." Thunder punctuated the younger brother's name.

Dooley was so engrossed in Jenny's words that he hardly noticed the water quickly rising in the hole. Now that she had stopped speaking, he saw that it had risen to his waist. Dooley looked at Jenny with eyes full of panic. "It's filling up. Help me!" he cried.

"This isn't real." Jenny was floating above the water. Her image was gradually fading into blurred lines.

"It feels real! It feels like I'm going to drown!" The water was at his shoulders now. Dooley dug into the dirt, feverishly snatching at the roots jutting out of the walls.

"But you won't drown." Jenny's voice was distant.

"Jenny, help me!" The water reached his nose. He prepared to hold his breath.

"Dooley."

As soon as Jenny said his name, Dooley was back in the rock lean-to, sitting cross-legged with his hands in his lap. Rain was falling on the flat rock above him. He opened his eyes and saw that he was alone. Jenny was gone.

FRIDAY

Thirty-Seven

A STITCH IN TIME

"It's our last full day at Camp Pukwudgee," said Busby from his perch at the base of the flagpole as he was closing out his morning announcements. "Let's make this the finest, friendliest, funnest Friday ever!" Busby dismissed the campers to their activities and the group dispersed.

Dooley was hardly paying attention to anything going on around him. Ever since he had left the Bloodstone Forest, all he could think of was trying to remember the version of the Waddle-dee-wop that Carrie had written on the back of a recipe card and read aloud to Peter.

"Dooley, did you hear me?" asked Cyrano.

Leo waved his hand in front of Dooley's face.

"Hello?"

"Oh, sorry," Dooley answered.

"I asked you if you still can't think of the rhyme," Cyrano said. He and Leo had both watched their friend toss and turn all night, struggling to remember the words.

"Nope. Every once in a while, I think I've almost got it—it's just on the tip of my tongue—then it's gone."

"Maybe you're trying too hard. Sometimes I find that the harder I try to remember something, the harder it is to remember," Leo offered. "And besides, you don't even know if it's an actual spell."

As the boys walked toward their cabin, Dooley reached for a piece of paper in the right back pocket of the shorts he'd worn the day before and felt the bloodstone still resting there. Choosing not to mention the stone to his friends and his negligence in delivering it, he withdrew the paper to read again and left the bloodstone in his pocket.

The creases in the paper showed it had been folded and re-folded several times. The three boys walked side-by-side along the path, reading what Dooley had written. "I think the last three lines are different than what we say now, but I just can't remember."

Hemmed in by rows of low rosebushes, the path narrowed. Looking down at his paper and consumed in his thoughts, Dooley veered too close and snagged his shorts on the thorns. His left back pocket was ripped off, creating a hole which revealed the underwear beneath.

"Oh, great!" he cried, slapping a hand over the hole.

Trying not to laugh, Leo filled his cheeks with air.

Cyrano looked at Dooley with amused sympathy. "We'll walk you over to the nurse's clinic," he said. "She can sew it."

Busby was sitting on the front porch of his cabin, looking at his clipboard, when he saw the boys heading to the nurse's clinic. "Can I help you, boys?" Busby asked.

"I tore my shorts on a rosebush, so I was hoping the nurse could fix them."

"She's gone to tend to some campers suffering from a bad case of poison ivy, I'm afraid," answered Busby. "But come on in, and I'll get you fixed up in a jiffy!"

The boys followed Busby into his cabin. As soon as Dooley stepped inside, he realized he'd been there before. He remembered the room from his time in Jenny's memory—the wallpaper, the burgundy rug, the coat tree—all just as he had seen it, except a painting above the fireplace mantle had been added and the petite green armchair by the window was gone. In its place, there was a leather recliner. Busby came out of a back room with a pair of pajama pants decorated with designs of railroad tracks and locomotives.

"Go change into these and bring me your shorts," Busby instructed. "There's a bathroom just on your left."

Dooley obeyed, slipping the paper and the bloodstone into one the pockets in the pajama pants, and returned to give Busby the torn shorts. Busby sat down in the leather armchair and lifted a sewing basket from the floor and onto his lap. Dooley gasped, "Oh!"

"I know what you're thinking, how did a guy like me—tough and manly—ever learn to sew?" Busby started.

"No, actually… Counselor Busby…" Dooley said.

"Well, I'm here to tell you fellas that these skills are for everyone. Anyone—man, woman or child—should know how to do these three things:

1. Sew a button.

2. Cook a spaghetti dinner.

3. Change a tire."

Busby licked the end of a piece of thread and squinted as he guided it through the eye in his needle.

"Counselor Busby..." Dooley tried again.

"There's so much in this great big world to learn about, boys! I have hundreds—yes, hundreds—of scout badges. I have one for cooking, one for motorboating, one for stamp collecting..."

"Counselor Busby!" Dooley said, louder than he had intended.

"Yes, Dooley?"

"I was wondering about your sewing basket."

Busby wore a look of surprise mixed with a slight irritation for being interrupted but handed the closed basket to Dooley anyway. "It's just an ordinary sewing basket," Busby said. "Wicker sides and a fabric, cushioned lid."

"Did it belong to anyone in your family?" Dooley asked, holding the basket in two hands.

"As a matter of fact, it did. It was my great-great grandmother's."

"Do you mind if I look inside?"

Busby grinned. "I also earned a badge for basket weaving, so I see you share my appreciation for the woven arts. Yes, please examine this fine example of an early 20th century sewing basket."

Dooley sat on the floor with his friends on either side of him. He slowly opened the lid and dug around in the basket's contents. He found spools of thread and various buttons, scissors and a little pillow stuck full of pins. His shoulders slumped when he realized that the recipe cards weren't there.

"I've just about finished mending the tear and reattaching your pocket, but your button here looks a little loose. I say we fix that little fella before you lose it. You know what they say, 'A stitch in time saves nine,'" said Busby as he reached for the scissors to cut his thread. "By the way, you can lift out the tray to find extra storage beneath."

Dooley brightened. With trembling hands, he took out the tray and set it on the floor. In the space below he found a delicate, white handkerchief with a *C* stitched in one corner and small bundle of notecards tied together with a strip of tattered blue ribbon.

Thirty-Eight

CUT YOUR THUMB

Dooley untied the ribbon from the stack of recipe cards and read through them, flipping each card over to look at the back. "There's a recipe for flapjacks, one for sourdough biscuits, one for prune pie…" Dooley made a disgusted face.

"Sounds delicious!" remarked Busby. "My great-great-grandmother was the cook for the logging camp here back in the early 1900's. I think these are her recipes."

Dooley continued looking at the cards. "Here's one for something called Booyah Stew." When Dooley flipped it over, he was relieved to see five lines printed neatly on the back. "Counselor Busby, do you have a pencil I could borrow to copy this down?"

"That stew does look appealing, doesn't it?" he said, assuming Dooley wanted to write down the recipe. Busby handed the mended shorts to Dooley and took the card, reading the ingredients for the stew aloud, "Short ribs and chicken. Cabbage, carrots, potatoes, and rutabaga. Yum!

You can use this." Busby took an ink pen from his shirt pocket. "This stew is more of a Fall recipe than one for summertime, but perhaps I could convince our head chef, Blanche, to give it a try in the camp kitchen."

Busby gave the card back to Dooley who had taken out the piece of paper from his pocket. "This recipe looks pretty difficult," said Dooley. "You have to cook it outside in a big pot called a *booyah kettle* over a fire for two days. I wonder if the kitchen cooks would be up for that."

"You may be right," Busby sighed.

"Don't give up yet," said Leo. "I bet Blanche would do just about anything you asked her to do."

"What do you mean?" asked Busby.

"Haven't you noticed? Blanche has a crush on you."

"Really?"

"Leo's probably right," offered Cyrano. "This mushy love stuff is his specialty."

Busby blushed slightly, stammering incoherently.

"Let me give you some advice," said Leo. "From my own experience, I've learned not to give up when you meet a girl that's really special, one you have a connection with."

Cyrano rolled his eyes. "Knock it off, Leo," he whispered, uncomfortably.

"You'll understand about love, someday, Cyrano…I hope." Leo put a hand on Cyrano's shoulder, which Cyrano promptly shrugged off.

"You're so weird," said Cyrano, shaking his head.

Dooley had finished writing the rhyme and returned the pen to Busby.

"Blanche and I have discussed our mutual fondness for mushrooms. Perhaps I could show her the most recent copy of *Fungus*, the magazine for mushroom enthusiasts that I subscribe to. I've got it somewhere…" Busby rifled through a pile of magazines and mail in a bin on the floor. "A-ha! Here it is! Just look at this beaut!"

Busby showed the boys the magazine. On the cover there was a picture of a stubby, peach-colored mushroom jutting out from a decaying piece of wood. In place of a mushroom cap there was a round, red spot at the top which looked just like a painted fingernail. "This is a *Xylaria pollicis*, also known as 'Dead Man's Thumb.'"

The boys listened politely, though they were ready to leave.

"It's said that when the thumb is cut, it gives off a very distinct aroma—a combination of buttered popcorn, rubber erasers and ginger snap cookies. Unfortunately, it tastes like rubber erasers, so it's not very appetizing to eat."

Dooley was looking down at the rhyme, specifically the phrase *Count to one and cut your thumb* while Busby described the mushroom. "Counselor Busby, are there mushrooms like that around here?" Dooley asked.

"As a matter of fact, there are," said Busby, cheerfully. "They can be found…"

"Deep in the Bloodstone Forest, I'm guessing?" Dooley interrupted, wearily imagining himself back in the forest for the third day in a row.

"No. I was going to say that I've sometimes found them by the fishing hole. There are rotted logs down there that are perfect cultivators for the Dead Man's Thumb."

"Thanks! You've been really helpful!" said Dooley as he walked to the door to leave.

"Dooley, aren't you forgetting something?" Busby asked, pointing to Dooley's legs.

Dooley looked down at the railroad pajama pants he was wearing and said, "Oh, yeah!" He went back to the bathroom and changed hastily, draping the pajama pants across the bathroom sink.

On the way to the fishing hole, Dooley asked Cyrano, "Can you use your olfa…"

"Olfavoyance?"

"Yeah, can you use olfavoyance to smell the future about these mushrooms? Are you getting any smells like the ones Counselor Busby said people notice when they cut a Dead Man's Thumb mushroom?"

Cyrano sniffed the air. "I'm getting the erasers and the popcorn…" *Sniff.* "Yes, and the ginger snaps, too."

"That's great!" said Dooley. "That means we're going to find it."

"And then what do we do with the mushroom after we cut it?" Leo asked.

"Well, I've got an idea," Dooley replied. "The second line goes, 'Waddle-dee-wop, faddle-dee-foo. Count to two and stir the brew.' I think the mushroom is an ingredient in the brew."

"Makes sense to me," agreed Leo.

Cyrano was sniffing again. "There's another smell, too. I can't place, it. Something like a feather pillow and maybe a sweaty sock full of old pennies, I think."

Dooley and Leo looked at Cyrano strangely. "Let's just concentrate on one thing at a time," said Dooley. "First, we've got to find that mushroom."

Thirty-Nine

STIR THE B.R.E.W.

Several yards downstream from the boat dock, there was a rocky shelf jutting out into the Hache River. Various trees and bushes hugged the area around the ledge, making it a shady spot perfect for fishing. Campers who had chosen fishing for their activity were sprawled around, lazily dipping their toes in the water. Tristen was the only one who seemed to care about actually catching anything. She was holding her pole in both hands and looking at the water intently, as if she was mentally taunting the fish to swim close to her fish hook.

"Let's keep it quiet," said Dooley. "We don't need everybody knowing what we're looking for and getting nosy." Cyrano and Leo nodded in agreement. The boys stooped as they hunted around the trees and undergrowth, searching for a mushroom that looked like a dead person's thumb poking out of dirt or decomposing wood.

"Dooley, over here," called Cyrano. "Is this it?" He pointed to a crumbling tree stump covered with a range of fungi. There were some that looked like seashells and some that looked like little tables. Right in the center, there was a cream colored mushroom shaped like a thumb.

"That looks just like the one in the picture," Dooley replied. "Now we need to cut it."

"Hang on," said Leo.

He ran over to where the fishing campers had set up and opened one of their tackleboxes. After rummaging inside, he returned to the stump with a pocketknife and a small plastic bag. "Here you go."

Dooley sliced the mushroom off at its base, releasing the odd odor Busby had told them about, and placed it in the plastic bag.

Cyrano sniffed the air. "There it is again—that feathery, sweaty, metallic smell."

"Are you worried about it?" Dooley asked.

"Maybe. It's just strange, that's all."

"Forget about the smell," said Leo. "How do we find the ingredients for the brew? It's like we need a cookbook or something."

"Leo, you're a genius!" Dooley exclaimed. "I've got a book that I think will give us the answer!"

Back in the Jackalope cabin, Cyrano and Leo watched as Dooley lifted the ordinary-looking, brown paper-covered textbook from under his bunk and held it in his lap. "When

Carrie wrote the second part of the rhyme, she wrote out the word *BREW* like every letter stood for another word," said Dooley. "Like how U.S.A. stands for the United States of America."

"So? Do you think that's important?" Leo asked.

"Maybe. I just want to be thinking about that when I ask this *Visus Encyclopedia* or whatever it's called to show me the recipe."

"Good idea," said Cyrano.

Dooley took a deep breath and opened the book. The title page read, *Toil and Trouble: A Beginner's Cookbook of Magical Mixtures by Julienne Saffron.* He flipped through the pages until he got to "Chapter One: Basic Brews." Dooley read aloud, "As most magical home cooks know, B.R.E.W. is a helpful acronym when creating a simple base. It's often called the béchamel sauce of enchanted concoctions. In equal parts, the chef should gather and prepare the following: powdered bark of a tamarack tree, ash from the root of a Blazing Bush (as opposed to a Burning Bush which has poisonous berries and should be avoided), one beaten egg of a Gowrow, and water. In other words, Bark, Root, Egg, Water. Mix these ingredients together, creating a smooth batter. Then continue with your recipe as instructed."

"Let's split up the ingredients to find them faster," said Dooley.

"I'll ask Counselor Boone where there's a Gowrow nest," said Leo, uncertainly. "I just have to remember about keeping unbroken eye contact and humming 'Camptown Races.'" Leo shuddered involuntarily. "Those lizards creep me out."

"I know where to find a Blazing Bush," Cyrano offered. "Calix showed it to me last year. It's behind the girls' latrine."

Dooley reached for his backpack and took out his enchanted compass. "And I'll use this to find the tamarack tree."

All of a sudden, something heavy crashed onto the cabin roof. They heard a scratching sound—metal against metal—and a loud screech. Dust was falling from the ceiling as the heavy creature pounded and scraped above them.

"Dooley!" Cyrano cried. "Did you ever put the bloodstone in the tree?"

"Oh, no! I totally forgot!" Dooley checked his pockets, as the pounding and screeching grew louder. "It's not here." He shook out his backpack and unzipped his sleeping bag, searching for the stone. Then he remembered, "I left it in the railroad train pajamas! It's in Counselor Busby's bathroom!"

"We've got to get out of here before the Snallygaster tears this place apart!" Leo yelled.

The boys peeked out the window and saw long, green tail feathers trailing along the ground. Then, one huge eye as big as a cantaloupe appeared with a curved beak on top. The upside-down, feathered face squawked angrily, blowing rancid breath through the window. The boys screamed and ran to the other side of the bunk room.

"Hey!" a voice called from outside. "Who's got one eye and bad breath?"

"You do, Metal Beak!" said a different voice.

"Who's that?" Dooley asked.

"It sounds like Tosh and Tot," Cyrano answered.

"Those crazy twins!" Leo cried. "They're gonna get killed! The Snallygaster doesn't like to be taunted."

The boys listened as the giant creature dismounted from the roof and landed in front of their cabin with a shriek that sounded like fingernails on a chalkboard. When they had halfway opened the cabin door, the boys saw the back of an enormous beast, nearly ten-feet tall. It had a the body of a lizard, but it had wings and was covered in feathers. Its razor-sharp claws looked like they were made of metal. Dooley, Cyrano and Leo watched to see what the twins would do next.

Tosh and Tut counted off together: "One… two… three!" Then they threw a large net over the ready-to-attack Snallygaster. The net was made of something red and sticky. The dragon-like bird wrestled and screeched, but the more it moved the more it flattened to the ground.

"Go!" said Tosh.

"Run!" said Tut.

Dooley, Cyrano and Leo threw open the door, slamming it against the wall as they dashed down the steps toward the twins.

"Thanks, guys!" said Leo.

"Yeah," Dooley said, breathing hard. "What is that net made of, anyway?"

"Red licorice ropes, of course," Tut answered, smiling.

"Everyone knows that a Snallygaster's one weakness is sugar," added Tosh. "It temporarily paralyzes him."

"Counselor Boone is teaching us everything about the creatures of Camp Pukwudgee," said Tut as he stroked the

Snallygaster's metallic-looking beak. The creature snapped at him irritably.

Tosh stuck out his chest proudly. "Someday maybe we'll be in charge of forestry and bee-keeping around here."

"And, if we're lucky we'll be Knitters, too." Tut stood up and put his hands on his hips. "You fellas ought to go finish the Waddle-dee-wop and put the bloodstone in the tree."

"We can't keep this critter tied up forever," Tosh warned them.

"Right," said Dooley, turning to his friends. "I'll go get the stone and the first ingredient. Then we'll meet back up at the cabin. Good luck!"

Forty

STEEP YOUR TEA

"Counselor Busby!" Dooley called as he pounded on the door of Busby's cabin. "Are you home?"

Dooley waited for a moment, then cautiously opened the door. He stepped over the threshold and into the room.

He called again, "Counselor Busby? Hello?"

Pausing to listen for any sounds in the cabin, Dooley looked around at the room. After he had determined that he was alone, he went to the bathroom. There he found the pajama pants just as he had left them. He reached into the pocket, took out the bloodstone and returned the pants to the sink. Then he dashed down the porch steps and ran all the way to the Bloodstone Forest.

Once he was back in the forest, Dooley took out his compass and said, "Show me which way to go to find the tamarack tree." The letters and needle spun around until the compass found its North, and Dooley took off in the direction of S.E.

It didn't take long for Dooley to realize that the compass seemed unsure where to send him. He'd hiked in the direction of the river, then the compass seemed to change its mind. Later, he'd found himself on the edge of the parking lot and the compass had changed again. The letters and needle would spin, and Dooley would have to go in a new direction.

With the steeple of the craft dojo looming before him at a distance, he stopped to re-check his bearings. Dooley heard a rustling behind him. He turned around quickly and realized he was face-to-face with Tristen.

"What are you doing here?" he asked, annoyed by another obstacle which might slow him down.

"Following you, obviously," she answered. "Although I think you have no idea where you're going."

"Just leave me alone, Tristen."

"Why? So you can cut up mushrooms and share recipes with your friends?"

Dooley started walking again. "Good grief. Don't you have anything better to do than follow me around?"

"Not really." Tristen walked beside him. "Plus, I think Counselor Busby will be pretty interested to know that you broke into his cabin. It might even get me a little closer to the triple P award."

"First of all, I didn't break into his cabin. I went in and got something I left there earlier today. Stop trying to make everything about getting that stupid award."

Tristen grabbed Dooley's arm and spun him around roughly. "It's not a stupid award!"

"Well, it's not as big of a deal as you think it is! I'm trying to do something important, so either help me find the tamarack tree or get out of my way!"

A shrill shrieking startled both of them. "Oh no!" Dooley said. "It's back."

"What's back?" Tristen asked.

Dooley was about to reply and tell her about the Snallygaster, but before he could get the words out of his mouth, the massive, winged creature flew down and snatched Tristen up by her shoulders. "Dooley! Help!" she cried, her legs kicking wildly in the air.

Momentarily frozen with panic, Dooley watched as the Snallygaster flew away. Instinctively, he looked down at his compass again and saw that it had determined S.E. was straight ahead. Deciding that the best way to appease the Snallygaster was to properly get rid of the bloodstone, Dooley rushed to find the tree.

In a few steps, he was standing before the same tall tree he had seen day before with the same light green needles and reddish pinecones. He hastily examined the tree and found a knothole. He placed the stone in the hole and read the Waddle-dee-wop from his scrap of paper.

Relieved, Dooley let out a deep exhale. He started to make his way back to the camp to find a counselor to tell about Tristen's capture by the Snallygaster, then he remembered his other reason for finding the tamarack tree. He pried a large section of bark from the tree and headed out of the forest.

Cyrano and Dooley laid out their ingredients and tools in the Jackalope cabin.

"I talked to Blanche in the kitchen," said Cyrano. "She let me borrow this bowl and spoon. She also let me borrow her cheese grater. I thought we could use it to make the bark into a powder."

"Great job," Dooley said. He started grating the bark over the bowl. "I hope Leo isn't having any trouble with the Gowrow egg."

"No kidding. I guess it would've been too easy for Julienne Saffron to just made this B.R.E.W. recipe out of butter, sugar and flour, huh?" Cyrano was using the pocketknife they'd found at the fishing hole to dice his ingredient into tiny pieces. "The Blazing Bush catches on fire every day at noon, so I was there just in time to dig out some roots before it went up in flames."

"I'm guessing the Blazing Bush grows back again?"

"Yep. It burns down to ash, then it sprouts and flowers before sunrise the next day."

Leo threw open the door and tumbled in, holding a large egg covered in purple speckles. "I got it!" he shouted triumphantly.

"What happened to you?" Dooley asked, pointing to the bandage on Leo's forehead.

"When I found the nest—I was down on my hands and knees, you know—I saw a Gowrow and got nervous. I couldn't remember what song I was supposed to hum, so at first I was humming 'Twinkle, Twinkle Little Star.' The Gowrow lunged at me, and its tusk scratched me up a little.

Then I remembered 'Camptown Races.' I stared it down and grabbed the egg and then I ran like crazy." Leo plopped down on the floor beside his friends. "I saw the nurse and she put this on my forehead."

"Very impressive, Leo," said Cyrano. "Seriously. I didn't know you had it in you."

"Thanks," Leo replied. "Oh and Dooley, the nurse told me about the Snallygaster and what happened to you and Tristen. She said to tell you that Counselor Boone is leading a search party to find her."

"I feel really bad about that," Dooley said. "If I had put the bloodstone away yesterday, none of that would've happened." Dooley cracked the egg over the bowl, adding it to the grated bark and diced root.

"As annoying as Tristen is, I feel bad for her, too," Cyrano admitted. "But if there's any camper here who can battle a ginormous dragon, it's her…and Tosh and Tut apparently." He poured water from a bottle into the bowl while Leo stirred.

Dooley lifted the book onto his lap and flipped through the pages. "So I found a recipe that starts with the basic B.R.E.W. batter, then you add sliced mushrooms. Let's try that with the Dead Man's Thumb we found by the fishing hole."

Cyrano sliced the mushroom into thin slivers and added them to the bowl. "Now what?" Cyrano asked.

"You have to let it set for a while. Maybe this is the part of the Waddle-dee-wop that says, 'Count to three and steep your tea.' We have to wait."

"But for how long?" asked Leo.

Dooley read further in the recipe. "It says you have to let it set for Fibonacci-16 minutes." He looked puzzled, then understanding brightened his face. "So if you count to the 16th place of the Fibonacci Sequence…"

"Fibonacci, the mathematician?" asked Leo.

"Yes, the 16th place of the Fibonacci Sequence is… 1, 1, 2, 3, 5, 8, 13, 21, 34, 55, 89, 144, 233, 377, 610, 987! We have to wait for 987 minutes!"

"Forget about fighting a Gowrow, that was actually more impressive!" Cyrano replied. "How in the world…"

"I'll explain later. Right now we need to figure out what time it will be in 987 minutes which is…" Dooley scribbled numbers on a piece of paper. "Almost 17 hours from now."

Cyrano looked at his watch. "It's nearly noon now, so the brew won't be ready until tomorrow morning, around 5:00."

Dooley covered the bowl with one of his t-shirts and slid it under his bed. "We might as well go eat lunch and start planning what to do for Number Four."

"And what is that?" asked Leo.

"Count to four and feed the shag boar," Dooley answered.

Forty-One

FEED THE SHAG BOAR

Dooley, Cyrano and Leo sat together as they ate their lunch in the mess hall. "I don't understand what a mathematician, dead thousands of years ago, has to do with anything," Cyrano said between bites of baked beans. "Is it just a coincidence that all of those things painted on the cave wall have the Fibonacci sequence design, *and* it was mentioned in the recipe?"

Dooley thought about it for a moment. "I don't know. I just keep thinking about the words that were written in the cave."

"Written by Peter," Leo offered.

"Right. The words Peter wrote on the cave walls. He wrote something like that without hope, the heart would break. And that you'll be all right if you can add a little more hopefulness to each day."

"Well, that's the Fibonacci Sequence," said Cyrano. "Adding more to what you already have until the numbers get really big."

"I think Peter was trying to help Jenny stay hopeful while he worked to find a cure. Maybe this stuff we're making will save her after all." Dooley looked down at his untouched plate of food and sighed.

Cyrano sniffed the air. "Something bad is coming this way," he said and sniffed again. "It smells like a pine tree that's been hosed down with caramel syrup."

"That doesn't sound too bad…" Dooley began.

"Where is he?!" All heads turned to see Tristen limping into the mess hall, making a beeline for Dooley. "You… you… idiot!" she screamed. Pinecones stuck out of her hair and pine needles were plastered all over her clothes and face. A branch stuck to her shoe and trailed along behind her. "They had to spray me with a sugar hose so that beast would drop me!" Her left eye twitched slightly. "Do you know what happens when you get covered in sticky sugar and fall onto a pine tree, Dooley?"

"Pine needles stick to you?" Dooley asked quietly.

"Yes! *Everything* sticks to you!"

Several campers in the mess hall choked back laughter. Dooley watched as flies swarmed around Tristen's head.

"Right now I've got to go to the nurse's clinic so that she can be sure I haven't broken any bones," she said through gritted teeth. "But I wanted to find you first to tell you that I'm not done with you yet." She leaned in to whisper in his ear. "You will pay for this."

Tristen swatted at the bugs as she stormed out of the mess hall.

"Bye, Tristen!" Cyrano called. "Thanks for stopping in!"

"There's something different about her," Leo said. "But I just can't put my finger on it."

"I think she's changed her hair," Dooley offered.

After lunch the boys went in search of Counselor Boone. Dooley had combed through his copy of *The Bloodstone Forest: A Field Guide*, but he couldn't find any mention of a shag boar, let alone what to feed it. Some of the campers told them that Boone was at the boat dock, so the three friends headed that way.

Once they had arrived, they found the director of water activities sorting through wet life jackets and hanging them on a rack. "Coach Penny," Dooley said, "Have you seen Counselor Boone? We have a wildlife question for him."

"Last I saw him was before lunch," she answered. "But I may be able to help you. What's your question?"

"Have you ever heard of a shag boar?" asked Dooley. "It's not in the field guide."

"You mean a Shagamaw Boar?" said Penny.

"Maybe," Cyrano said. "Are there any around here?"

"That's hard to say." Penny stepped over to the rows of canoes and began wiping them down. "No one's seen a Shagamaw Boar in all the years I've been here, at least not a live one."

"But it's something that used to exist?" Dooley asked.

"Supposedly. They're big, hairy hogs that walk on hind

legs like people. They live in ornately-decorated, under-ground caverns. They mate for life. The female never goes outside, and the male species is forever searching for any-thing that might make its burrow more comfortable for its mate."

"Have you ever seen a picture of a Shagamaw Boar?" Leo questioned.

"As a matter of fact, I've seen something better than a picture. A few summers ago when we were cleaning up after camp was over, we re-organized the attic of the meeting lodge. We found a stuffed Shagamaw Boar up there."

"Like a stuffed animal?" asked Dooley.

"Like a dead one that's been preserved through taxidermy. It's not in the best condition, but it's about as accurate as you're going to get."

The boys thanked Coach Penny and left the dock.

"Leo, do you think you can paint a picture of the boar?" Dooley asked as they walked toward the lodge.

"I can try," Leo said. "Once I see the stuffed one, I'll know better."

The attic of the lodge was spacious and well-lit by the sun coming in the two small windows that looked out to the yard in front. The hardwood floors were covered with colorful area rugs in geometric designs from the Southwest. The ceiling was slanted, the highest point a ridge running down the center. Stacks of labeled boxes lined the back wall, and in the middle of the room there were mountains of the kind of miscellaneous items collected over several decades, such as numerous lamp shades, two sewing cabinets and a full-body bee-keeping suit with veil hood.

The boys spread out to find the stuffed boar, shifting piles and lifting sheets of canvas cloth. They stirred up dust and knocked down cobwebs. A few times, Dooley found something so interesting he had to remind himself the purpose of their search and keep looking.

Eventually, Cyrano called out, "I found it!" and the boys joined him a dark corner. In his hand, Cyrano victoriously held a floral shower curtain which moments before had been draped over a hairy figure standing nearly as tall as him. It had brownish-black fur, small ears, two stubby tusks and a black snout. Patches of the fur had been rubbed away on its belly and one cheek. Its front hooves were split like a pig's and its back hooves were rounded like a horse's. The animal was mounted on a wooden platform with a small gold plaque displayed in the center. The plaque read, "The Mighty Shagamaw Boar—1952."

Dooley looked at the boar's little glass eyes. They were black, and along with the slight smile on its face, they somehow gave the animal a friendly expression. Dooley smiled back and said, "Let's get this guy to the craft dojo."

Forty-Two

LEARN TO SHRIVE

Leo connected four large painting canvases together to make one giant canvas. "I have to paint the boar the size we want it to be in real life," he told Dooley and Cyrano. Then apart from an occasional *hmm*, Leo silently walked around the boar, examining it in precise detail.

"This will probably take a while. Leo doesn't like to be rushed," Cyrano whispered. "Why don't we go figure out the last line while he's working." Dooley agreed, and the boys walked back to their cabin.

Once inside the Jackalope cabin, Dooley checked on their B.R.E.W. He noticed the surface was covered with bubbles, and it was emitting a sour smell. Supposing this was a desirable state for the resting magical batter, Dooley slid the bowl back under his bed and retrieved the *Cantata Liber*.

"The last line of Carrie's Waddle-dee-wop goes: 'Count to five and learn to shrive,' so I'm going to ask the book to tell me what *shrive* means," he said.

Dooley opened the book and read the title page aloud—
Dictionary of Words Twelve-Year Old Boys Almost Never Say.
"That is surprisingly accurate," Cyrano replied.

Dooley flipped to the back of the book to the S-section.
"Schlump, shadoof, shaveling… ah, here it is… shrive. It
means 'to hear or make a confession' or 'to receive forgiveness by confessing.'"

"So is Jenny supposed to hear a confession or confess to
something so she can be forgiven?" asked Cyrano.

Dooley sat with the question, staring at the book in his
lap but not really seeing the words. He was thinking about
the memories Jenny had shared with him—the night she
convinced her brother Caleb to punish Whispering Dan
by scaring him, resulting in Dan's death, Jenny and Caleb
remaining forever in their magical forms, Peter's loss of
his powers and their mother Carrie's heartbreak. Dooley
finally answered, "I think Jenny is supposed to make a
confession. I think we're supposed to make the brew, feed
it to the Shagamaw Boar, and then Jenny is supposed to
admit what she's done and say she's sorry."

"Okay," Cyrano replied. "Then let's go find Sama and see
if she'll help you tell all of this to Jenny."

Dooley and Cyrano found Sama sitting alone on the front
porch steps of the Wendigo cabin. She wore headphones
and leaned back against the top step with her eyes closed
and her face tilted towards the sun. She was humming softly.

Dooley touched Sama's arm to let her know they were

there. "Oh, hey guys," she said as she took off her headphones. "Sometimes all of the noises get to be too much, and I just have to block them out. What's up?"

"I was wondering if you could help me talk to Jenny again, like we did in the forest."

"Do you know where she is?" Sama asked.

"No, but I was thinking I'd look in the places I've seen her before. Maybe start by the mess hall then over to that big rock near the parking lot—"

"Then back to the Bloodstone Forest?" Sama asked apprehensively. "It's going to be dark soon."

"Yes, if it comes to that," Dooley answered. "But I'm hoping we'll find her before we have to go to the forest."

"Dooley has this spell—well, it's an older version of the Waddle-dee-wop," Cyrano explained. "And we think that a part of helping Jenny and her brother Caleb is for Jenny to admit what she's done wrong."

"That is after Leo paints a Shagamaw Boar into real life and we feed it a nasty soup we made using a mushroom that looks like a dead thumb." Dooley realized just then how ridiculous it all sounded when he said it out loud.

Sama rose to her feet and stretched. "So the mess hall first?" she asked.

They wandered around the grounds surrounding the mess hall, but Dooley never saw any sign of Jenny and Sama didn't hear her. Then they walked through the parking lot and followed Snallygaster Road until they saw the big rock where

Dooley had first spotted Jenny at the beginning of the week.

"There she is!" Dooley exclaimed. Jenny was sitting with her ankles crossed and her hands bracing her on each side. She was looking down, her long braid fell across one shoulder. "Jenny!" called Dooley before he had reached the rock. "I need to talk to you!"

Jenny's mouth moved and although he couldn't hear what she was saying, Dooley knew she was sad.

"Jenny says she knows that tomorrow is Saturday and you'll be leaving," Sama said. "And she's sorry she hasn't been able to find you today. She was very tired after sharing her memories with you yesterday."

"That's okay," Dooley said. "I understand. I wanted to tell you about an idea I have. I think it might help."

Dooley told Jenny about the recipe card and the mushroom and the B.R.E.W. and the Shagamaw Boar. He told her about the book only a Visus could read and how it defined the word *shrive* in a way that made him believe she had an important role in helping to free her brother and herself.

"Assuming our plan works and the seeds are reversed," said Dooley, "what do you think will happen to you and Caleb?"

"I think I will finally be able to rest," Jenny said through Sama, "and Caleb will also find his peace. Living past your 100th birthday is only a blessing if you can share your every-days with people you love, not cold and lonely, made of wind and shadows."

"The B.R.E.W. will be ready early in the morning, just before sunrise," Dooley told her. "Meet me at the flagpole then, and Jenny… be ready to shrive."

SATURDAY

SPAR TREE

It was still dark outside when Dooley, Cyrano and Leo crept out of their cabin and sprinted to the craft dojo. Leo slid open the rice paper door as quietly as he could. Sensei Elenore slept in the cabin several buildings down with the other female counselors, but they weren't taking any chances of getting caught. Their mission was too important.

As soon as they were inside, the boys heard a scuffling sound coming from the kitchen. Rifling through the upper cabinets was a 6-foot tall boar covered in coarse, brown hair. He was standing on skinny hind legs and had his snout stuck in a box of cereal. When the creature saw them, he froze and the boys did the same. The cereal box slowly slid off his snout and onto the floor, leaving multi-colored rings stuck to his tusks and mouth.

"It worked," Leo said, both pleased and shocked. "It really worked. I painted the boar and now it's standing in the dojo kitchen eating Rainbow Rounds cereal."

"Leo, it's huge," said Cyrano. "How in the world are we supposed to get it to the flagpole?"

"I've thought of that." Leo tapped his temple and winked his eye. "Leonardo Rembrandt Johnson comes with a plan in hand. Coach Penny said the male Shagamaw Boar is always looking for something to give his lady so that she'll be more comfortable in their underground cavern." The boar had lost interest in the boys and turned his attention to a jar of peanut butter he was awkwardly trying to open with his cloven hooves. "So I asked Counselor Boone to knit something a Shagamaw Boar might like."

"Okay," said Dooley. "And he didn't think that was weird?"

"Maybe, but he really appreciated my combined interest in knitting and forestry animals, so he did it." Leo went to a different room and came back with bright yellow, knitted blanket. Stitched throughout the design were pink daisies with glittery yarn used for the center of each flower.

When the boar saw the blanket, he dropped the peanut butter jar and walked toward Leo as if in a trance. "I'll get him over to the flagpole," said Leo as he walked backwards slowly.

"Okay," said Dooley. "I'll go find Caleb."

Cyrano looked at his watch. "I'll get the B.R.E.W. from the cabin—I think it's steeped enough now."

Dooley looked at his friends. "Let's meet at the flagpole as soon as we can and hope that Jenny is there, too."

Dooley remembered seeing a dog bed on Busby's front

porch, so he decided that was the best place to look for the Golden Retriever early in the morning. Just as he had hoped, he found Caleb snoozing peacefully. Dooley approached him cautiously, aware of the danger of waking a sleeping animal.

"Caleb," Dooley whispered. "Wake up, boy." Caleb growled but remained motionless with his head down and eyes closed. "Caleb," Dooley said a little louder. "It's time to wake up. We're going to help you and Jenny."

Caleb raised his head and barked, causing Dooley to stumble down the porch steps.

"Now you've made him angry." Dooley saw a boy coming around the corner.

"Virgil!" Dooley said. "What are you doing out so early in the morning?"

"I could ask you the same thing."

"Well, I was…"

"Let me stop you right there, dude," said Virgil. "Because I don't really care." Virgil started to walk away. "I'm working on vocabulary for crepuscular animals—ones that are active at dawn and dusk. There's a bobcat that roams around here that has a slight Canadian accent, and I'm dying to record it for translation."

"Wait!" Dooley called. "Help me talk to Caleb. I've got to get him to come to the flagpole with me right now."

Virgil huffed irritably but walked back to the porch. He barked and yipped a few times and Caleb barked back.

"Caleb just told me that he doesn't want to go to the flagpole with you, especially if his sister is going to be there."

"Tell him that we have a plan. We're going to help him undo what happened to him all those years ago."

Virgil barked some more and Caleb responded with one long growl.

"He said *no*."

"Then tell him that I know about Whispering Dan and the seeds. Tell him that Jenny is sorry. Tell him that his mother would want them to make this right."

Virgil relayed Dooley's message and waited for Caleb's reply. Eventually the dog barked and yipped and growled and howled and whined for several minutes. Virgil translated Caleb's message as he spoke:

When I was a boy, my mother was our spar tree. Do you know what that means? That's the tallest, strongest tree that all the other trees are attached to. That was our sweet mother. She was everything to us kids after Pa died. We broke her heart that night, but she never gave up on us. On the day Momma died, we lost our spar tree, our balance, our grip. I will go with you if you think that's what Momma would want.

Forty-Four

SUNRISE AT THE FLAGPOLE

When Dooley and Caleb arrived at the flagpole, the sun was just beginning to peek out and color the morning. Scanning the assembled group, he saw Cyrano holding the t-shirt-covered bowl and Leo near the Shagamaw Boar who was dreamily rubbing the yellow, knitted blanket against his hairy cheek. Sama and Clio sat on the base of the flagpole. Caleb sat down next to them and laid his head on his paws, sleepily.

"I hope it's okay that we came, too," said Clio. "Considering Sama is a part of your crew."

"Yeah, I didn't want to miss this," Sama said. "Is Jenny here?"

"No. I don't see her," said Dooley, discouraged.

"Well, why don't we go ahead and start feeding the B.R.E.W. to the boar?" Cyrano suggested. "It may take a while, especially if he doesn't like it."

"Come here, Shaggy," Leo said, as he attempted to convince the boar to sit on the ground. "It's breakfast time."

Cyrano handed Leo the spoon and uncovered the bowl. A nauseating smell wafted up from the soupy, gray concoction. Leo took the bowl from Cyrano and scooped up a lumpy spoonful. The boar sniffed it and leaned away.

"Open up, Shaggy. Yummy-yum! Who's a hungry Shagamaw Boar?" Leo tried to get the spoon into the boar's mouth, but the animal wouldn't cooperate. He kept his lips tightly closed and grunted.

"Try flying the spoon as if it were a plane or chug it along like it's a choo-choo train," Clio offered. "What? It worked when my mom fed Celeste as a baby. He might go for it. You never know…maybe."

Leo took her advice, but the boar was adamant in his refusal. His lips remained closed.

"That's just great. The boar won't eat. Jenny's not here," Dooley grumbled. "I had to work hard to convince Caleb to come. I had to promise him that this was what his mom would want."

Cyrano patted Dooley on the back, consolingly. "Don't give up. Remember what Peter wrote on the cave walls?"

Dooley thought for a minute then said, "Hope has two beautiful daughters. Their names are Anger and Courage—Anger at the way things are, and Courage to see that they do not remain as they are."

"Right," said Cyrano. "Let's stay focused on what we're trying to do. Carrie wrote those words to the Waddle-deewop for a reason."

"You're right," Dooley agreed. "Clio, did I tell you Jenny's mom was a Rhymer? She may have never really called herself that, but in all of the memories Jenny shared with me, her mom spoke in rhymes, and she loved poetry."

"Do you have the original rhyme from Jenny's mother?" Clio asked. "I'd like to read it, from one Rhymer to another."

"I have it written down on a piece of paper in my cabin. I'll run back and get it."

Dooley hurried to the Jackalope cabin and quickly found the paper. Just as he had shut the door and started down the cabin steps, he thought he saw Jenny out of the corner of his right eye standing at the edge of the Bloodstone Forest. As he hustled past Busby's cabin, Jenny disappeared into the darkness.

"Jenny!" Dooley called. "Wait!" He rushed in after her, stumbling over the rutted forest floor, until he found her back at the rock lean-to where they had sat together the day she had shared her memories. Dooley stooped to enter the squat space and sat down across from her. She mouthed the word *hollow*, and Dooley dissolved into Jenny's memory.

TREE OF LIFE

Dooley and Jenny stood in the doorway of a modest bedroom. Carrie—frailer now than the last time Dooley had seen her—lay under a quilt in a four-poster bed. Peter sat in a chair next to her, stroking her hair. "Momma, how are you feeling?"

"Old, worn and teary, but mostly just weary." Carrie smiled, weakly.

"Well, we're going to get you better. You just take it easy, and I'll look after you."

A Golden Retriever rested its chin on the opposite side of the quilt and looked at Carrie with sad eyes. Dooley searched for the other Jenny—the one who had experienced the original memory—and found her sitting on the floor by a dresser, hugging her knees.

"What is it you always say about hope?" Peter asked, gently. "Build hopefulness adding a little more to what you had the day before. Don't give up, Momma."

"Hope delayed makes the heart sick with strife, but a dream fulfilled is a tree of life." Carrie said, "The Book of Proverbs, chapter 13, verse 12. Look it up if you don't believe me, there's a Bible on the shelf."

"I believe you, Momma. You have the best memory of anyone I know. Oh, that reminds me!" Peter reached inside the breast pocket of his suit coat and took out a small box. He opened the box and showed Carrie what was inside. "One of the camp counselors made this for you. It looks like an ordinary blue button, but it's been charmed with a spell. It can take you back to any memory."

Carrie halfheartedly reached for the button and held it in her open hand. "Dreams are like memories in a fog. They can be as finicky as a Shagamaw Hog."

"I don't understand what you mean."

"The Shagamaw Boar likes sweet food. Now that I'm old, I like memories that way, too." Carrie gave the button back to Peter, and he laid it on the bedside table.

"Don't you have any memories you'd like to revisit? They can't have all been bad. Some of them must've been sweet."

"Remembering in color wears me out these days. I lack the strength to give my memories more than tints of gray." Carrie closed her eyes. "Let me dream, son. Death's clock has won." She drew in one ragged breath, then she was still.

"Momma?" Peter stood up, jostling the bedside table and knocking the button onto the floor. He felt her wrist for a pulse. Realizing his mother was gone, he sat back down, held his head in both hands and wept inconsolably.

Dooley watched the button roll under Peter's chair and across the room, until it slipped in between two floorboards and became lodged there.

A woman came in the room. She was pressing one hand to the small of her back and the other hand rubbed her growing belly. "Peter? Are you okay?"

Peter grabbed the woman's hand. "Momma passed on."

"Oh, darling, I'm so sorry." She kissed the top of his head.

"There's nothing to keep us here now," Peter told her. "Let's leave the camp and move away. This place holds too much sadness for me, and I want our child to be born somewhere happier."

The Jenny standing in the doorway said, "I was wrong, and my family suffered for it. I'm ready to go with you now. It's time, Dooley." As soon as she said his name, Dooley was transported back to the forest where they were sitting knee-to-knee inside the lean-to.

On the way to the flagpole, Dooley snuck in to the mess hall to grab a few packets of sugar. When they got to the group, Cyrano was trying to pry open the boar's mouth, and Leo was desperately singing, "I like to eat, eat, eat apples and bananas."

"Let's make the B.R.E.W. sweeter," Dooley said, handing Cyrano the packets of sugar. "I heard once that a Shagamaw Boar likes his food sweet."

They sprinkled the sugar on top and set the bowl on

the ground. The boar lapped it up, hungrily. Caleb was awake now and watching the scene from his perch on the uppermost section of the flagpole base. Jenny went to stand next to him.

Dooley handed the piece of paper with the Waddle-dee-wop to Clio. She read it aloud:

Waddle-dee-wop, ploddle-dee-plum!

                        Count to one and cut your thumb!

Waddle-dee-wop, faddle-dee-foo!

                        Count to two and stir the brew!

Waddle-dee-wop, beedle-dee-bee!

                        Count to three and steep your tea!

Waddle-dee-wop, noodle-dee-nor!

                        Count to four and feed the shag boar!

Waddle-dee-wop, chiddle-dee-chive!

                        Count to five and learn to shrive!

Dooley looked toward the flagpole, watching for any sign that their efforts had been successful. The sun was right behind Caleb and Jenny. Dooley had to squint as he stared into the bright light. He rubbed his eyes, and when he opened them again, the girl and the dog were gone.

Forty-Six

THE SQUONK

Dooley, Cyrano and Leo rolled up their sleeping bags and repacked their duffels.

"I still can't believe I got this," Leo said as he gazed appreciatively at the wooden plaque in his hands.

It was inscribed with gold letters that Dooley read aloud, "PERFECT PUKWUDGEE PARTICIPANT: We completely communicate that this camper has exhibited an exemplary example of Pukwudgee pride, propriety, and principles."

"You can always tell when Counselor Busby is excited about something," Cyrano said. "He starts using alliteration a bunch."

"This really should've been yours, Dooley," Leo told him. "I mean, you were the one who figured everything out to help Jenny and Caleb."

"But you did the magical painting," said Dooley, "And when Busby found out that you made a female Shagamaw

Boar to go with the male one, he was pretty impressed."

"Beneath that red polo shirt beats a heart yearning for romance," Leo said.

"Yeah, and it didn't hurt that you were the one who told Busby about Blanche, the kitchen cook who has a crush on him," Cyrano said. "I heard they have a date tonight in town."

The boys lugged their bags to the Jackalope front porch and waited for their parents to pick them up.

Solemn-faced, Tristen strode purposefully to their cabin, stopping just a few feet from the porch steps. "Congratulations, Leo. You definitely didn't deserve it, but whatever… blah, blah, blah."

"Uh, thanks," Leo responded warily. "I think."

"Dooley, can I talk to you for a minute?" she asked.

Dooley stepped off the porch hesitantly and approached her.

"Listen, not getting the P.P.P. plaque has really got me thinking, and I wanted to apologize if I've been mean to you. Sama and Clio told me about Jenny and how she needed to confess stuff to get forgiveness and find peace. I know I can be a little competitive sometimes…"

"A little?" Dooley began.

"Okay, more than a little. So anyway—sorry."

Dooley was so surprised by Tristen's apologetic declaration that he was speechless and could only watch her walk away. As he was standing with his mouth open, spellbound by her speech, Dooley noticed a creature burrowing under a hedge by the path. It looked like a possum if its skin were three sizes too big for its body and covered in warts.

"Leo… Cyrano…" Dooley called as loudly as he dared so as not to frighten the creature. "Come see this. I think it's a Squonk."

Leo and Cyrano joined Dooley. "Yep, that's it," whispered Leo. "Let's follow it. It's supposed to lead you to things you've lost."

The boys crept along as the Squonk crawled under the hedges. Eventually, the creature came to the steps of Busby's cabin. The front door was wide open, and the animal slunk inside. When the boys saw him again, he was rooting around in between the floorboards of Busby's bedroom.

As soon as Dooley saw what the Squonk was after, he gasped, "It's the button."

The frightened Squonk instantly melted into a puddle on the floor. As the liquid slowly trickled out of the room, Dooley reached down and picked up the ordinary-looking, blue button.

"What's the big deal?" Leo asked.

"Yeah," said Cyrano. "It's just a button."

Dooley gazed down at the object in his hand. "You never know. Sometimes ordinary things turn out to be something pretty special. And anyway, with the summer almost over and school starting soon, a little bit of magic may just be what I need." Dooley slid the button into his shorts pocket. "It feels good to have something to hope for!"

ABOUT THE AUTHOR

Abby Rosser makes her home in Murfreesboro, Tennessee with her husband and four kids. She enjoys reading, watching movies, baking (and eating) desserts and being outside—but not all at the same time.

And she loves imagining stories (often when's she's doing most of the above).

Find out more about Abby at abbyrosser.com.

Also by Abby Rosser

Believe

Also available from WordCrafts Press

The Awakening of Leeowen Blake
    by Mary Garner

Tears of Min Brock
    by J.E. Lowder

Summer on the Black Suwannee
    by Jennifer Odom

You've Got It, Baby!
    by Mike Carmichael

The Mirror Lies
    by Sandy Brownlee

www.WordCrafts.net

www.ingramcontent.com/pod-product-compliance
Lightning Source LLC
Chambersburg PA
CBHW050529190726
48284CB00003B/1001